ALI CONCERT

MW00330752

Book, Words and Music by

Elizabeth Swados

SAMUEL FRENCH, INC.

45 WEST 25TH STREET   NEW YORK 10010
7623 SUNSET BOULEVARD   HOLLYWOOD 90046
LONDON   *TORONTO*

PUBLIC THEATER VERSION

MUSICAL NUMBERS
ACT I

What There Is* .... Meryl
The Rabbit's Excuse .... Mark & Co.
Down Down Down .... Meryl, Betty & Co.
Drink Me .... Deborah, Rodney, Michael, Stuart & Co.
Good-By Feet .... Meryl & Co.
The Rabbit's House .... Michael, Amanda, Mark & Co.
Bill's Lament .... Michael & Men
Caterpillar's Advice .... Richard & Co.
Beautiful Soup .... Meryl
Wow Wow Wow .... Sheila & Co.
Pretty Piggy .... Meryl & Co.
Cheshire Puss .... Rodney & Meryl
If You Knew Time .... Betty & Co.
No Room No Room .... Richard, Mark, Michael, Meryl & Co.
Starting Out Again .... Meryl & Co.
White Roses Red .... Stuart, Michael, Rodney & Deborah
Alphabet .... The Company
Red Queen .... Deborah & Co.
Never Play Croquet .... Meryl & Co.
Mock Turtle Lament .... Mark, Deborah & Meryl
The Lobster Quadrille .... Richard, Betty & Co.
Eating Mushrooms .... Meryl & Co.

ACT II

Child of Pure Unclouded Brow .... Deborah, Stuart
Jabberwocky .... Richard & Co.
Humpty Dumpty .... Meryl & Co.
Tweedledum & Tweedledee .... Michael, Stuart
The Walrus & The Carpenter .... Charles, Amanda & Co.
The White Queen .... Meryl
The White Knight .... Mark & Meryl
An Aged, Aged Man .... Meryl & Mark
The Lion & The Unicorn .... Sheila
What There Is* .... Rodney, Meryl, Richard
Queen Alice .... The Company
What Is A Letter .... Meryl, Betty & Co.

THERE WILL BE ONE TEN-MINUTE INTERMISSION.

UNDERSTUDIES: For Alice—**Deborah Rush;** For The Women—**Kathryn Morath;** For The
Men—**David Patrick Kelly & Pi Douglass.**
Back-up Singer: **David Patrick Kelly**
*Based on the poem by Kenneth Patchen
Courtesy of New Directions, All Rights Reserved

Production Supervisor for
the New York Shakespeare Festival
Jason Steven Cohen

6

ALICE AT THE PALACE

Alice At the Palace, a 90-minute adaptation of Elizabeth Swado's *Alice in Concert*, was broadcast on January 16, 1982, on the NBC Television Network.

Meryl Streep starred as Alice, with Debbie Allen, Betty Aberlin, Stuart Baker-Bergen, Richard Cox, Sheila Dabney, Rodney Hudson, Michael Jeter, Charles Lanyer, Mark Linn-Baker, Kathryn Morath, Deborah Rush, and Carolyn Dutton. Elizabeth Swados wrote the 26 songs in the program. Emile Ardolino directed, Graciela Daniele choreographed the dances, and Theoni V. Aldredge designed the costumes. "Alice At the Palace" is a Joseph Papp/New York Shakespeare Festival Production.

A BRIEF HISTORY

Lewis Carroll is one of the most noted and quoted authors of children's books who ever lived. His classics, *Alice's Adventures in Wonderland* and *Through the Looking Glass*, are available in over 40 languages, making them two of the most translated books in the world. Although they were originally written for children, Carroll's books have proven to be perennial favorites of readers of all ages.

Why are these stories about a little girl's adventures so popular? Many reasons have been given. Literary critics have cited the author's obvious love for children and his remarkable ability to convey their view of life. Carroll provided a clue when he identified the basic theme of the stories as "the idea of change" — both physical and emotional. The Alice books have endured because they provide a portrait of the experience of growing up. They are also fascinating excursions into the world of dreams.

Over the years, *Alice's Adventures in Wonderland* and *Through the Looking Glass* have been the source for numerous animated films, musicals, and stage productions. This new presentation is a pageant of movement, songs, dances, and mime. It invites viewers to return to the wonderful world of play to experience once again the surprises, the word games, and the riddles of Lewis Carroll's imagination.

A NOTE FROM THE AUTHOR

Alice in Concert is the first in a series of what I call "concert-dramas" to be brought to the stage. When we first performed it at the Public Theatre, our set was a semi-circle of folding chairs and large cardboard vaudeville signs denoting the title of each chapter. Someone rang a bell, someone changed the sign, and presto! — we were in a new part of Wonderland. The blocking consisted basically of standing up and sitting down, with an occasional dance or two. This approach had an extraordinary effect because the audience could hear the old and beloved text and watch fine actors in street clothes transform their spirits into classic characters. Visual stereotypes or "original interpretations" did not impede the childlike imagination in anyone. Thus, as in African dance drama, storytelling, or Brazilian samba, whole mythologies can be covered with little or no costume, make-up or affect.

My *Alice in Concert* has evolved into a slightly more elaborate rendition, but the core of the style remains true. Try first to stage an unusual, precise, presentational concert with Alice literally wandering through the singers and musicians, *then* add choreography and slight characterization if you wish. But avoid elaborate sets or blocking. Let voices, pitch, change in musical style and intonation dictate the intensity of a moment. This is the way to stay true to my original intention.

Of course, a director may, if he or she wishes, follow the specific staging that goes with our text, but each company brings its own talents and quirks, and I say if the Catepillar plays the harmonica, put it in! If the Duchess is a juggler, let her juggle pans and plates. If the Red Queen is a break dancer, all the more power to her/him. The main goal is to stay true to the music, to move at a lightning pace, and to avoid all clichés of children's theater or "experimental" imagistic theater. Let the words be put out there. This is an old idea, but new in this age. The concert transforms; the performers become guides through a musical world. Think of the *Histoire du Soldat* or *Peter and the Wolf*. Open up the concert to fine acting values, but don't try to make a play. The only progression is Alice's increasing illumination and growth. Her wisdom and ladylikeness. Her growing generosity. This is the actress' heavy responsibility and must be carried off with the simplicity of a folksong.

Elizabeth Swados
October 2, 1986

9

COMPANY

(original cast in alphabetical order)

WOMAN 1, EDITH .... Betty Aberlin
MAN 2, TWEEDLEDUM, TEA TABLE .... Stuart Baker-Bergen
MAN 5, MAD HATTER, JABBERWOCK,
    CATERPILLAR............................... Richard Cox
WOMAN 2, DUCHESS, A QUEEN .... Sheila Dabney
MAN 1, CHESHIRE CAT, UNICORN............. Rodney Hudson
MAN 3, BABY, BILL, DORMOUSE, TWEEDLEDEE ....Michael Jeter
MAN 4, LION.............................. Charles Lanyer
WHITE KNIGHT, MOCK TURTLE, WHITE RABBIT,
    MARCH HARE .... Mark Linn-Baker
WOMAN 5 .... Kathryn Morath
WOMAN 4, PAT .... Amanda Plummer
WOMAN 3, RED QUEEN, GRYPHON .... Deborah Rush
ALICE, HUMPTY DUMPTY, WHITE QUEEN .... Meryl Streep

MUSICIANS .... David Conrad, Carolyn Dutton, Judith Fleisher,
      Robert J. Magnuson, David Sawyer, William Uttley,
                        Tony Viscardo

MUSICAL CUES

ACT ONE

1. OVERTURE OF BELLS – "WHAT THERE IS"
2. EXCUSE ME (The Rabbit's Excuse)
3. DOWN, DOWN, DOWN
4. DRINK ME
5. GOOD-BYE FEET
6. DIALOGUE
7. THE RABBIT SENDS IN A LITTLE BILL
8. BILL'S LAMENT
9. ADVICE FROM A CATERPILLAR
10. BEAUTIFUL SOUP
11. WOW! WOW! WOW!
12. PRETTY PIGGY
13. CHESHIRE CAT
14. IF YOU KNEW TIME
15. NO ROOM (The Tea Party)
16. LEARNING TO DRAW
17. STARTING OUT AGAIN
18. WHITE ROSES RED
19. DIALOGUE BEFORE THE ALPHABET
20. THE ALPHABET
21. THE RED QUEEN
22. NEVER PLAY CROQUET
23. THE MOCK TURTLE'S STORY
24. THE LOBSTER QUADRILLE
25. EATING MUSHROOMS

ACT TWO

26. CHILD OF PURE UNCLOUDED BROW
27. JABBERWOCKY
28. HUMPTY DUMPTY
29. HUMPTY DUMPTY CHORALE
30. TWEEDLEDUM AND TWEEDLEDEE
31. THE WALRUS AND THE CARPENTER
32. THE WHITE QUEEN
33. THE WHITE KNIGHT
34. AN AGED, AGED MAN
35. THE LION AND THE UNICORN
36. WHAT THERE IS (Reprise)
37. QUEEN ALICE
38. WHAT IS A LETTER?
39. BOWS

11

Alice in Concert

ACT ONE

The entire COMPANY enters from different locations at the exits and the back of the audience. Each has a "Swiss Bell." (Tones used are A, B, C, C# low, C# high, D low, D high, E, F# low, and G.) Depending on the number of cast members, one member or more could have two bells.

[MUSIC NO. 1: OVERTURE OF BELLS — "WHAT THERE IS"]

After the houselights blackout, a light shines on the CONDUC-TOR who cues the orchestra and then conducts the COM-PANY in the OVERTURE. At Bar 13, the tempo changes to very fast. The CONDUCTOR continues to conduct, the lights begin to come up, and the COMPANY, playing their bells, walk to the performance area. By Bar 25 they are lined up in a row in front of the orchestra platform; ALICE is in the center with EDITH to her right. They sit on the edge of the platform and place the bells behind them.

During Bars 26 and 27 ALICE assumes a relaxed position, lean-ing against EDITH with her feet up on the platform.

ALICE.
IN THIS MY GREEN WORLD
FLOWERS, BIRDS ARE HANDS
THEY HOLD ME
I AM LOVED ALL DAY . . .

ALL THIS PLEASES ME
I AM AMUSED
I HAVE TO LAUGH FROM CRYING . . .
TREES MOUNTAINS ARE ARMS
I AM LOVED ALL DAY . . .

CHILDREN GRASS ARE	EDITH. (*above singing*)
TEARS	Alice was beginning to get very
I CRY	tired of sitting on the bank,
I AM LOVED ALL DAY . . .	and of having nothing to do;

13

EVERYTHING POMPOUS
  MAKES ME LAUGH
I AM AMUSED OFTEN
  ENOUGH
IN THIS MY BEAUTIFUL
  GREEN WORLD
OH THERE IS LOVE ALL
  DAY.

once or twice she had peeped into the book her sister was reading, but it had no pictures or conversations in it, and "what is the use of a book," thought Alice, "without pictures or conversations?" (*EDITH's speech is timed to end simultaneously with ALICE's song.*).

ALICE. (*in unison with EDITH*) So she was considering in her own mind (as well as she could, for the hot day made her feel very sleepy and stupid), whether the pleasure of making a daisy chain would be worth the trouble of getting up and picking the daisies, when suddenly . . .

So she was considering in her own mind . . . (*EDITH drops out.*)

(*The WHITE RABBIT, a cast member wearing rabbit ears, stands up from the platform and scurries across the playing area.*)

WHITE RABBIT. Oh my ears and whiskers, I shall be late!

[MUSIC NO. 2: EXCUSE ME — THE RABBIT'S EXCUSE]

(*The WHITE RABBIT continues to scurry around, followed by ALICE as he sings. The rest of the COMPANY remains seated on the platform.*)

RABBIT.
YOU'LL JUST HAVE TO
EXCUSE ME . . .
I AM IN A
FIT OF HURRY . . .
I MAY NOT
REMEMBER A THING
  TODAY.
YOU'LL JUST HAVE TO

COMPANY.

EXCUSE HIM.

OH, DEAR ME.

HE'S FORGOTTEN

EXCUSE ME.	'SCUSE HIM.
YOU MAY HAVE TO	YOU MAY HAVE TO
LOOK THE OTHER WAY.	LOOK THE OTHER WAY.
I AM JUST SO	I AM JUST SO
PIQUED WITH MYSELF	PIQUED WITH MYSELF
TODAY	TODAY.
THERE'S NO	THERE'S NO,
TELLING WHAT I	HE'S NOT HIMSELF
MIGHT DO OR SAY.	HE'S NOT HIMSELF TO-
	DAY.
YOU'LL JUST HAVE TO	
EXCUSE ME	YOU'LL JUST HAVE TO
I AM IN AN	EXCUSE HIM.
INCREDIBLE HURRY.	HE IS IN AN
YOU'LL JUST HAVE TO	INCREDIBLE HURRY.
EXCUSE ME.	YOU'LL JUST HAVE TO
I AM IN AN	EXCUSE HIM
INCREDIBLE HURRY.	HE IS IN AN
	INCREDIBLE HURRY.

RABBIT & COMPANY.
DOESN'T LIFE MAKE YOU VERY LATE
WHEN YOU ARE LOOKING ALL AROUND,
DOESN'T LIFE MAKE YOU VERY LATE
WHEN YOU ARE LOOKING ALL AROUND,
ALL A-A-AROUND.
  RABBIT.
I'LL BE LATE.
THERE IS SO MUCH TO SEE.
  COMPANY.
WHEN YOU LOOK.
  RABBIT.
THERE IS SO MUCH TO HEAR.
  COMPANY.
WHEN YOU LISTEN.
  RABBIT.
THERE IS SO MUCH TO SMELL
  COMPANY.
WHEN YOU SMELL
  RABBIT.
TO TELL.

COMPANY.
WHEN YOU TALK.
RABBIT.
PLACES TO GO.
COMPANY.
WHEN YOU WALK.
RABBIT.
THINGS TO KNOW
COMPANY.
WHEN YOU THINK.
RABBIT.
LOTS TO DRINK.
COMPANY.
WHEN YOU DRINK.

RABBIT.	COMPANY.
AND SO ON, AND SO ON,	AH AH
AND SO ON, AND SO ON.	AH AH.

I'LL BE LATE
RABBIT & COMPANY.
YOU'LL JUST HAVE TO EXCUSE ME
I AM SO DELIGHTED BY ALL THE THINGS I SEE
BUT I MAY NEVER GET TO WHERE I'M SUPPOSED TO BE
I AM IN AN INCREDIBLE HURRY
YOU'LL JUST HAVE TO EXCUSE ME.
RABBIT.
I AM IN AN INCREDIBLE HURRY
COMPANY.
HE'S LATE NOW

RABBIT.	
YOU'LL JUST HAVE TO	COMPANY.
EXCUSE ME.	EXCUSE ME.

RABBIT & COMPANY.
DOESN'T LIFE MAKE YOU VERY LATE
WHEN YOU ARE LOOKING ALL AROUND
DOESN'T LIFE MAKE YOU VERY LATE
WHEN YOU ARE LOOKING ALL AROUND
ALL A-A-AROUND.

(*RABBIT scurries off. ALICE gives up chasing him. She returns
    to the platform and starts carefully walking along its edge
    mumbling to herself.*)

ALICE. Excuse me . . . Excuse me . . .

(*ALICE suddenly loses her balance and stumbles off the platform. She is falling down the Rabbit Hole. Slide whistle indicates falling. She spins slowly, her arms waving, then collapses onto her back, and begins waving her arms and legs in slow motion as if she is suspended in air. The COMPANY remains seated on platform.*)

[MUSIC NO. 3: DOWN, DOWN, DOWN]

ALICE. Either this well is very deep or I'm falling very slowly. (*She continues to wave her arms and legs in the air.*)

EDITH. (*sings*)
ISN'T THE WORLD . . .
ALICE. Well, after such a fall as this . . .
EDITH.
SO VERY STRANGE . . .
ALICE. I shall think nothing of tumbling downstairs.
EDITH.
FIRST I WAS DOWN . . .
ALICE. How brave they'll think me at home!
EDITH.
NOW I'M DOWN FURTHER . . .
ALICE. Why I wouldn't say anything about it even if I fell . . .
EDITH.
I AM FALLING . . .
ALICE. . . off the top . . .
EDITH.
I CAN'T SEE TOP . . .
ALICE. . . off the top of the roof.
EDITH.
I CAN'T SEE BOTTOM . . .
ALICE. (*sung*)
ISN'T TIME . . .
EDITH. I wonder how many miles I've fallen . . .
ALICE.
SO CHANGEABLE?
EDITH. . . by this time?
ALICE.
FIRST I'M HERE . . .

EDITH. I must be getting somewhere near the center of the earth.

ALICE.
AND THEN I'M NOT . . .

EDITH. Let me see: that would be four thousand miles down, I think . . .

ALICE.
I'VE BEEN TRAVELING SO LONG . . .

EDITH. Yes, that's the right distance.

ALICE.
AND NOT ARRIVING.

COMPANY. (*sung*)
DOWN. DOWN. DOWN.
THERE'S NOTHING ELSE
  TO DO.
I'M JUST FOLLOWING
GRAVITY
IT'S BIGGER THAN ME OR
YOU . . .

ALICE. (*spoken*) Dinah! My kitty shall miss me very much tonight, I should think.
(*sings:*)
I HOPE THEY REMEMBER
HER SAUCER OF MILK
AT TEA TIME.
DINAH MY DEAR.

EDITH.
ISN'T IT COLD . . .

ALICE. I wish you were down here with me.

EDITH.
FALLING THROUGH AIR . . .

ALICE. There are no mice in the air, but there may be bats.

EDITH.
THINKING YOU'VE LANDED . . .

ALICE. And they're very like mice, you know.

EDITH.
BUT YOU'RE NOT THERE.

ALICE. But do bats eat cats?

EDITH.
THERE IS NO UP.

ALICE. Or do cats eat bats?

EDITH.
THERE IS NO DOWN.

ALICE. Do bats eat cats?

EDITH.
I AM FALLING.

MEN.   ALICE. (*sings*)
HOW LONG HAVE I
BEEN UPSIDE DOWN?   OOOOOO . . .
IT'S RIGHT SIDE UP
TO ME.
  COMPANY.
HOW LONG WILL I   OOOO . . .
STAY IN THE AIR?
  ALICE.
IT'S GETTING LONELY.
  WOMAN 1.
DOWN.
  MAN 1.
DOWN.
  WOMAN 2.
DOWN.
  ALICE.   COMPANY.
HAVE I BEEN GOING   OOOO . . .
  YEARS THIS WAY?
  COMPANY.   ALICE.
WHEN I REACH WHERE   OOOO . . .
  I'M FALLING TO
  ALICE & EDITH.
WILL ANYONE BE THERE TODAY?

  EDITH. (*sings*)
IT IS SO SAD
  ALICE. Ooooooooooo.
  EDITH.
FALLING THROUGH SPACE
  ALICE. Ooooooooooo.
  EDITH.
WITH NO OTHER VOICES
NO OTHER FACE.
  COMPANY.
IT'S BEEN SO LONG
THAT I'VE BEEN FALLING
OOOOOOOOOOOOOOO   ALICE. (*speaks*) I guess I'll
                         keep falling.

(*The Bass plays a sliding note to indicate falling, which ends with
    a loud boom on the bass drum. ALICE's feet and hands slap*

to the floor to suggest that she's landed. Four cast members [MAN 1, MAN 2, MAN 3 and WOMAN 3] stand up and move over to examine her. She stands up and brushes herself off.)

ALICE. (*speaking to herself*) I must have gone through the center of the earth and come out where the people walk upside down. The Antipathies, I think. (*to WOMAN 3*) Excuse me, ma'am, is this Australia or New Zealand?

[MUSIC NO. 4: DRINK ME]

(A vial of liquid descends from above the stage and stops in front of ALICE's face.)

MEN 1, 2 & 3. (*enticing ALICE to take vial*)
DRINK ME.
WOMAN 3.
READ THE LABEL DEAR.
MEN 1, 2 & 3.
OH, DRINK ME.
WOMAN 3.
JUST BE CAREFUL, DEAR.
MEN 1, 2 & 3.
DON'T LISTEN TO A WORD YOUR MOTHER SAID,
DRINK ME.
WOMAN 3.
JUST DON'T DISOBEY.
MEN 1, 2 & 3.
DRINK ME.
WOMAN 3.
THAT COULD MAKE YOU ILL.
MEN 1, 2 & 3.
OH, DRINK ME.
WOMAN 3.
READ THE LABEL, DEAR.
MEN 1, 2 & 3.
IT'S BEAUTIFULLY PAINTED ON MY COVER,
NOW DRINK ME.
MAN 2.
WHAT WERE THE WORDS YOUR MOTHER SAID
WHEN SHE SAID

WOMAN 3. (*speaks in rhythm*)
"Do not drink out of bottles marked poison."
Children get burnt and eaten by beasts
If they do not listen to the simple rules
that are taught them.
  COMPANY. (*sings*)
YOU MAY CUT YOUR FINGER VERY DEEPLY WITH A
  KNIFE
AND IT WILL BLEED.
ALSO IF YOU HOLD A RED HOT POKER VERY LONG
YOU WILL BE BURNED.
SO DRINK ME.
ENJOY ME.
DON'T YA WORRY 'BOUT A THING . . .
  ALICE. (*speaks*) I'll just have a little taste. (*She grabs the vial and drinks a little, then chugs the whole thing down.*)

  MAN 1. (*sings*)
I TASTE LIKE . . .

  ALICE. (*speaks in rhythm*)
Custard.
Bananas.
Hot buttered toast.
Cherry tarts, pineapple,
Turkey and toffee.
  COMPANY. (*speaks in rhythm*)
Custard.
Bananas.
Hot buttered toast.
Cherry tarts, pineapple,
Turkey and toffee.

Hot buttered toast.
Hot buttered toast.
Hot buttered, hot buttered,
Hot buttered toast.
Cherry tarts, pineapple,
Turkey and toffee.
  MAN 4. (*in a deep voice*)
Drink me!

(*ALICE begins to react to the drink. She makes exploding noises with her throat; her arms and legs jerk out to give the impression that she's getting bigger. She sits down with her feet straight out in front of her and remains this way during the next song. The CAST returns to the platform and sits.*)

ALICE. Now I'm opening up like the biggest telescope there ever was!

[MUSIC NO. 5: GOOD-BYE FEET]

ALICE.
GOOD-BYE FEET.
COMPANY.
GOOD-BYE ALICE.
ALICE.
OH, MY POOR LITTLE FEET.
COMPANY.
OH, POOR ALICE.
ALICE.
I WONDER WHO'LL PUT ON YOUR STOCKINGS AND
    SHOES.
COMPANY.
WE WONDER WHO WILL WALK WITH YOU.
ALICE.
I'M SURE I WON'T BE ABLE.
COMPANY.
WE'RE SURE YOU WON'T
    BE ABLE.   ALICE.
WE SHALL BE A GREAT   I SHALL BE A GREAT
    DEAL   DEAL
TOO FAR OFF   TOO FAR OFF
TO TROUBLES OURSELVES   TO TROUBLE MYSELF
    ABOUT YOU.   ABOUT YOU.

ALICE.
YOU MUST MANAGE THE BEST YOU CAN.
COMPANY.
BUT WHO WILL TIE OUR SHOELACES, OH!
ALICE.
YOU MUST MANAGE THE BEST YOU CAN.

COMPANY.
BUT WHO WILL PULL UP OUR SOCKS? OH!
ALICE.
YOU MUST MANAGE THE BEST YOU CAN.
(*speaks in rhythm:*)
But who will bring me home at tea time?
COMPANY.
YOU MUST MANAGE THE BEST YOU CAN
ALICE.
But who will bring me down on Christmas morning?
COMPANY.
YOU MUST MANAGE THE BEST YOU CAN.
ALICE.
In this situation I think that—
ALICE & COMPANY.
WE MUST MANAGE THE BEST WE CAN.
ALICE.
Good-bye Feet.
COMPANY.
BYE BYE!

(*ALICE stands up and wanders around as if lost.*)

[MUSIC NO. 6: DIALOGUE]

ALICE. (*musical intro vamps under*) Dear Dear! How queer
everything is today! And yesterday things went on just as usual.
I wonder if I've been changed in the night? Let me think: *was* I
the same when I got up this morning? I almost think I can
remember feeling a little different. But if I'm not the same, the
next question is, "Who in the world am I?" Ah, *that's* the great
puzzle! (*sings*)
I'M SURE THAT I'M NOT ADA
FOR HER HAIR GROWS IN SUCH SHORT RINGLETS
AND MINE DOESN'T GO IN RINGLETS AT ALL.
AND I'M SURE THAT I'M NOT MABLE
FOR I, I KNOW ALL SORTS OF THINGS
AND SHE, OH SHE KNOWS SUCH A VERY LITTLE.
(*Guitar continues vamping.*)
(*speaks:*) Besides, *she's* she and *I'm* I, and, oh dear, how puz-
zling it all is! I'll try if I know all the things I used to know. Let me

see: (*She sings.*)
FOUR TIMES FIVE IS TWELVE,
AND FOUR TIMES SIX IS THIRTEEN,
AND FOUR TIMES SEVEN IS . . .
(*Guitar continues vamping.*)
(*speaks:*) Oh dear! I shall never get to twenty at that rate.
However, the multiplication table doesn't signify. Let's try
geography, shall we? (*She sings.*)
LONDON IS THE CAPITAL OF PARIS
AND PARIS IS THE CAPITAL OF ROME
AND ROME . . . (*Guitar stops.*)
(*speaks:*) No, that's all wrong, I'm certain. I must have changed
for Mabel! I'll try and say "How Doth The Little Crocodile."
(*She assumes recitation pose and begins.*)

How doth the little crocodile
Improve his shining tail
And pour the waters of the Nile
On every golden scale.

How cheerfully he seems to grin.
How neatly spreads his claws,
And welcomes little fishes in
(*Her voice begins to get scratchy and low.*)
With gently smiling jaws!

I'm sure those are not the right words. I must be Mabel after all,
and I shall have to go and live in the White Rabbit's pokey little
house forever.

(*A large dollhouse is brought to center stage. Throughout the
following dialogue ALICE plays with the dollhouse, stick-
ing her hands and fingers in windows, arranging furniture,
etc. Behind her CAST MEMBERS carry on conversation
punctuated by percussion sound effects. The dialogue is
spoken very quickly.*)

[MUSIC NO. 7: THE RABBIT SENDS IN LITTLE BILL]

RABBIT. Mary Ann! Mary Ann!
WOMAN 3. It's the White Rabbit!
RABBIT. Fetch me my gloves this moment!
WOMAN 1. He's taken me for his housemaid!
RABBIT. Then I'll go 'round and get in at the window. Oh,
what's there? Pat! Pat! Where are you?

PAT. Sure then I'm here! Digging for apples, yer honour.

RABBIT. Digging for apples, indeed! Here! Come and help me out of this! Now tell me, Pat, what's that in the window?

PAT. Sure, it's an arm, yer honour!

RABBIT. An arm, you goose! Who ever saw one that size? Why, it fills the whole window! Well, it's got no business being there at any rate. Go and take it away.

PAT. Sure I don't like it, yer honour, at all, at all!

RABBIT. Do as I tell you, you goose. (*He slaps PAT.*)

PAT. Ahhhhhh!

RABBIT. Where's the ladder? Bill's got to go down the chimney.

BILL. I ain't goin.'

COMPANY. Oh yes you are.

BILL. I said I ain't goin'.

COMPANY. Oh yes you are.

BILL. I said I ain't goin'.

COMPANY. Yes you are.

BILL. Looks like I'm goin.'

(*The COMPANY picks up BILL and simulates putting him down a chimney. At the dollhouse, ALICE does same with a miniature doll, and then throws the doll up in air. BILL is tossed up in air by the COMPANY.*)

RABBIT. Catch him you by the hedge!

MAN 1. Hold up his head.

MAN 5. Brandy now.

MAN 2. Don't choke him.

MAN 4. How was it old fellow? What happened to you?

ALICE. Tell us about it, Bill.

(*The MEN and BILL gather like a Barbershop Quartet.*)

[MUSIC NO. 8: BILL'S LAMENT]

BILL. (*blows pitch on pitchpipe and sings*)
I'M MINDING MY OWN BUSINESS
MEN.
BUSINESS . . .
BILL.
WHEN DOWN THE CHIMNEY I DID GO.

MEN.
HE GOES DOWN . . .
BILL.
THEN SOMETHING COMES AT ME LIKE A JACK IN A
  BOX.
MEN.
HMMMMM MMMMMM . . .
BILL.
AND UP LIKE A SKY-ROCKET I DID GO.
MEN.
AND DOWN IN THE HEDGE GOES HIS NOSE . . .
BILL.
GOES MY NOSE.

BILL & MEN.
AND HE IS MINDING HIS OWN BUSINESS
AS DOWN THE CHIMNEY HE GOES.
AND SOMETHING COMES AT HIM
SOMETHING COMES LIKE A JACK IN A BOX
AND UP HE GOES, AND UP HE GOES.

COULD YOU HELP HIM SIT UP A BIT BOYS?
OLD BILL'S HAD A BIT OF A BLOW.
DOING HIS DUTY FOR DOUBLE-U RABBIT
AND UP LIKE A ROCKET HE GOES.
AND UP LIKE A ROCKET HE GOES.
AND DOWN IN THE HEDGE GOES HIS NOSE.
GOES HIS NOSE.

(*The CAST begins to set up scene for the CATERPILLAR
    sequence under ALICE's next dialogue.*)

ALICE. No, I've made up my mind about it: if I'm Mabel, I'll
stay down here! It'll be no use their putting their heads down and
saying, "Come up again, dear!" I shall only look up and say,
"Who am I, then? Tell me that first, and then, if I like being that
person, I'll come up: if not, I'll stay down here till I'm somebody
else." But, oh dear! I do wish they *would* put their heads down!
I'm so *very* tired of being all alone here! I must be growing small
again. But then, shall I *never* get any older than I am now?
That'll be a comfort one way—never to be an old woman. But
then always lessons to learn! Oh, I shouldn't like *that*!

[MUSIC NO. 9: ADVICE FROM A CATERPILLAR]

(*The MEN have arranged themselves on a ladder to look like a Caterpillar's body. The MAN at top of ladder provides the Caterpillar's voice. OTHERS are seated on rungs below him to look like segments of his body. All move their arms and hands in undulating manner to look like Caterpillar's legs. MAN playing the BABY is positioned at bottom of ladder as the last segment of the Caterpillar's body. He has a bowl on his head. Both BABY and bowl will be utilized at the end of the song. WOMEN sing from offstage along with MEN.*)

COMPANY.
WHO ARE YOU? WHO ARE YOU? . . . (*They continue to sing this throughout the entire number, under the ALICE and CATERPILLAR dialogue.*)

CATERPILLAR. (*sung in Indian raga style; draw out as long as wished.*)
WHO . . . ARE . . . YOU?

ALICE. I hardly know, sir, just at the present. At least I knew who I was when I got up this morning, but I think I must have been changed several times since then.

CATERPILLAR. (*Raga style*)
WHAT DO YOU MEAN BY THAT?
EXPLAIN YOURSELF.

ALICE. I can't explain myself, because I'm not myself, you see? And being so many different sizes in a day is very confusing.

CATERPILLAR. (*Raga*)
IT ISN'T.

ALICE. Well, it is to me.

CATERPILLAR. (*Raga*)
YOU. WHO ARE YOU?

ALICE. (*disgusted, she answers him Raga style*)
I THINK YOU OUGHT TO TELL ME WHO YOU ARE
FIRST.

CATERPILLAR. Silence! (*The COMPANY stops singing.*) I've something important to say to you.

ALICE. What?

CATERPILLAR. Keep your temper.

COMPANY. Ahhhhhh!

ALICE. Is that all?
CATERPILLAR. No!

(*Pause, then a two bar musical introduction.*)

COMPANY.
ONE SIDE WILL MAKE YOU GROW TALLER.
THE OTHER SIDE WILL MAKE YOU GROW SHORTER.
ONE SIDE WILL MAKE YOU GROW TALLER.
THE OTHER SIDE WILL MAKE YOU GROW SHORTER.
ALICE. (*speaks in rhythm*)
One side of what?
The other side of what?
CATERPILLAR. The mushroom!

(*A GONG is sounded. At same time ALICE hits the bowl sitting on top of the BABY's head with a spoon. In the original production, ALICE took the bowl off the BABY's head and struck it again establishing her pitch for next musical number. The rest of the CAST gets off the ladder and sits at opposite sides of the playing area. ALICE sits down next to the BABY who is sprawled on the floor in a daze.*)

[MUSIC NO. 10: BEAUTIFUL SOUP]

ALICE. (*sings, holding bowl and spoon and feeding the BABY*)
BEAUTIFUL SOUP,
SO RICH AND GREEN
WAITING IN A HOT TUREEN.
WHO FOR SUCH DAINTIES WOULD NOT STOOP?
SOUP OF THE EVENING, BEAUTIFUL SOUP.
SOUP OF THE EVENING, BEAUTIFUL SOUP.
ALICE & COMPANY.
BEAUTIFUL SOUP!
BEAUTIFUL SOUP!
SOUP OF THE EVENING,
BEAUTIFUL, BEAUTIFUL SOUP!

ALICE. (*sneezes*) There's too much pepper in that soup!

[MUSIC NO. 11: wow! wow! wow!]

(*The COMPANY is seated on opposite sides of the playing area. Each member has a pot, pan, or percussion instrument which is beaten at points indicated in the score. The DUCHESS and the CHESHIRE CAT step forward to address ALICE when they sing. Alice stays seated with the BABY. She protects him every time the DUCHESS lunges at him.*)

DUCHESS.
SPEAK ROUGHLY TO YOUR LITTLE BOY
AND BEAT HIM WHEN HE SNEEZES.
HE ONLY DOES IT TO ANNOY,
BECAUSE HE KNOWS IT TEASES,
IT TEASES,
BECAUSE HE KNOWS IT TEASES.
    COMPANY.
WOW, WOW, WOW!
WOW, WOW, WOW!
WOW, WOW, WOW!
WOW, WOW, WOW!
    BABY. (*sings jazz scat in high whiny voice*)
DUBA DUBA DUBA BA
DUBA DUBA DUBA BA
DUBA DUBA DUBA BA
DUBA DUBA DUBA DUBA
BA

    COMPANY. (*sings*)
OOO . . . OOO . . . OOO . . .
OOO . . . OOO . . . OOO . . .

    ALICE. (*speaks in rhythm*)
Why does your cat
grin like that?
    DUCHESS. (*speaks in rhythm*)
It's a Cheshire Cat,
and that's why, Pig!

    COMPANY. (*chants in rhythm*)   CHESHIRE CAT. (*sings*)
HUA DAKA DAKA DAK!   MEOW

HUA DAKA DAKA DAK!	MEOW
HUA DAKA DAKA DAK!	MEOW
HUA DAKA DAK!	MEOW

ALICE. (*speaks in rhythm*)
I didn't know that Cheshire cats could grin.
In fact I didn't know that cats could grin.
    DUCHESS. (*speaks in rhythm*)
They all can
and most of them do!

COMPANY. (*chants in rhythm*)	CHESHIRE CAT. (*sings*)
HUA DAKA DAKA DAK!	MEOW
HUA DAKA DAKA DAK!	MEOW
HUA DAKA DAKA DAK!	MEOW
HUA DAKA DAK!	MEOW

ALICE. (*speaks in rhythm*)
I don't know
any that do.
    DUCHESS. (*speaks in rhythm*)
You don't know much and
and that's a fact.

COMPANY. (*chants in rhythm*)	CHESHIRE CAT. (*sings*)
HUA DAKA DAKA DAK!	MEOW
HUA DAKA DAKA DAK!	MEOW
HUA DAKA DAKA DAK!	MEOW
HUA DAKA DAK!	MEOW

ALICE. (*speaks in rhythm*)
Mind what you're doing!
Mind his precious nose!
    DUCHESS. (*speaks in rhythm*)
If everybody minded their own business
The world would go 'round faster than it does.

COMPANY. (*chants in rhythm*)	CHESHIRE CAT. (*sings*)
HUA DAKA DAKA DAK!	MEOW
HUA DAKA DAKA DAK!	MEOW
HUA DAKA DAKA DAK!	MEOW
HUA DAKA DAK!	MEOW

ALICE. (*speaks in rhythm*)
That would not be an advantage.
It takes twenty-four hours
for the world to go 'round
on its axis.

COMPANY. (*chants in rhythm*)
TALKING OF AXES, CHOP OFF HER HEAD!
KI KI KI KI
KI KI KI KI
KI!

DUCHESS. (*sings*)
I SPEAK SEVERELY TO MY BOY
AND BEAT HIM WHEN HE SNEEZES
FOR HE CAN THOROUGHLY ENJOY
THE PEPPER WHEN HE PLEASES,
HE PLEASES,
THE PEPPER WHEN HE PLEASES.

COMPANY.
WOW, WOW, WOW!
WOW, WOW, WOW!
WOW, WOW, WOW!
WOW, WOW, WOW!

BABY. (*improvises scat singing in high whiny voice*)
EH, EH, EH, EH, EH,
EH, EH, EH, EH, EH,
etc.

(*At end of scat the BABY starts to choke and ALICE burps him.*)

DUCHESS. O.K., you nurse him for awhile.

[MUSIC NO. 12: PRETTY PIGGY]

(*COMPANY remains seated on sides. ALICE cuddles the BABY.*)

ALICE.
IF I DON'T TAKE

COMPANY.
IF I DON'T TAKE
   ALICE.
THIS CHILD AWAY FROM THEM
   COMPANY.
OW!
   ALICE.
THEY ARE SURE TO KILL IT IN A DAY OR TWO.
   BABY. (*speaks*)
Don't kill me!

ALICE.	BABY. (*snorts in rhythm*)
EVEN THOUGH IT SNORTS AND IT	SNORT, SNORT, SNORT, SNORT
GRUNTS ALL THE TIME	SNORT, SNORT, SNORT, SNORT
I DON'T THINK THAT THAT'S A PROPER	SNORT, SNORT, SNORT, SNORT
THING TO DO.	SNORT, SNORT, SNORT, SNORT

   COMPANY. (*speaks*)
You're so right!
   ALICE & COMPANY. (*sings*)
WHY DOES EVERYTHING I HOLD
TURN INTO SOMETHING ELSE?
   ALICE.
SHUT UP, BABY, YOU SOUND LIKE A PIG,
SNORTING AND GRUNTING AND PORKLING AND
  SNORKLING.

   COMPANY.
SHUT UP BABY, OR I'LL MAKE YOUR TAIL UNCURL.

   ALICE & COMPANY.
OH WELL, IT'S BETTER TO BE
   ALICE.
A PRETTY LITTLE PIGGY THAN A
POKEY LITTLE BOY!
   COMPANY.
OW!
   ALICE.
THOUGH I CAN IMAGINE

IF I THINK HARD AND LONG
   ALICE & WOMEN.
THAT THERE ARE LOTS OF LITTLE GIRLS
WHO'VE TURNED OUT WRONG,
WITH EMPTY LITTLE HEADS AND
OVERSIZED FEET.
WHO CAN'T DO SUMS CORRECTLY
OR KEEP THEIR DRESSES NEAT.
   ALICE & COMPANY.
OH WELL, IT'S BETTER TO BE
A PRETTY LITTLE PIGGY
THAN A POKEY LITTLE GIRL.
   ALICE.
LIKE MY SISTER, EDITH.

(*The CHESHIRE CAT is located either behind a post in the
theater or at the back of theater. Throughout the number he
keeps moving around appearing and disappearing. ALICE
stays at center stage.*)

CAT. Mieow!

[MUSIC NO. 13: CHESHIRE CAT]

   ALICE. (*sings*)
CHESHIRE PUSS . . .
   CAT. Mieow? (*The CAT stealthily approaches her.*)
   ALICE.
WOULD YOU TELL ME PLEASE . . .
   CAT. What?
   ALICE.
WHICH WAY I OUGHT TO GO FROM HERE?
   CAT.
THAT DEPENDS A GOOD DEAL ON WHERE
YOU WANT TO GET TO.
   ALICE.
I DON'T MUCH CARE WHERE.
   CAT.
THEN IT DOESN'T MATTER WHICH WAY YOU GO.
   ALICE.
SO LONG AS I GET SOMEWHERE

CAT.
OH, YOU'RE SURE TO DO THAT
IF YOU ONLY WALK LONG ENOUGH.

ALICE.
WHAT SORT OF PEOPLE LIVE AROUND HERE?

CAT.
IN THAT DIRECTION, LIVES A HATTER
AND IN THAT DIRECTION LIVES A MARCH HARE.
VISIT EITHER YOU LIKE, THEY'RE BOTH MAD.

ALICE.
I DON'T WANT TO GO AMONG MAD PEOPLE.

CAT.
OH, YOU CAN'T HELP THAT.
WE'RE ALL MAD HERE.
I'M MAD. YOU'RE MAD,
I'M MAD, YOU'RE MAD.
I'M MAD.
YOU'RE MAD.

ALICE. How do you know that I'm mad?

CAT.
YOU MUST BE OR YOU WOULDN'T HAVE COME HERE.

ALICE.
AND HOW DO YOU KNOW THAT YOU'RE MAD?

CAT.
TO BEGIN WITH, A DOG'S NOT MAD,
YOU GRANT THAT?

ALICE.
I SUPPOSE SO.

CAT.
WELL THEN, YOU SEE, A DOG GROWLS
WHEN IT'S ANGRY
AND WAGS IT'S TAIL
WHEN IT'S PLEASED.
NOW I GROWL WHEN I'M PLEASED
AND WAG MY TAIL WHEN I'M ANGRY.

	ALICE.
THEREFORE I'M MAD!	THEREFORE YOU'RE MAD!

COMPANY.
HATTER OR MARCH HARE ⎫
HATTER OR MARCH HARE ⎪ (*sing 5 times*) (*ALICE and*
HATTER OR MARCH HARE ⎬ *CAT dance a*
HATTER OR MARCH HARE ⎭ *wild jitterbug.*)

HATTER OR MARCH HARE

CAT. Do you play croquet with the Queen today?

ALICE. I haven't been invited. Yet.

CAT. You'll see me there. (*CAT disappears. He can hide behind posts in the theater or slip down behind a row of seats. He reappears in another section of theater.*) By the by. Whatever became of the baby? I'd nearly forgotten to ask.

ALICE. He turned into a pig. (*CAT disappears again, then reappears.*)

CAT. Did you say PIG or FIG?

ALICE. P . . P . . Pig. And I wish you would stop doing that.

CAT. What?

ALICE. Appearing and disappearing. It makes me very giddy.

CAT. All right. (*CAT disappears again, and then reappears grinning broadly.*)

ALICE. Well! I've often seen a cat without a grin, but a grin without a cat! That's the most ridiculous thing I've ever seen!

COMPANY.
HATTER OR MARCH HARE
HATTER OR MARCH HARE   (*sing 5 times*) (*ALICE and*
HATTER OR MARCH HARE   *CAT do*
HATTER OR MARCH HARE   *another jitter-*
                                          bug.)

HATTER OR MARCH HARE!
WHICH WAY TO GO?

CAT. (*over music*) You're on your own, kid. (*He exits.*)

[MUSIC NO. 14: IF YOU KNEW TIME]

(*During the following song WOMAN 1 stands at one side with a megaphone and shouts out each line before it is sung.*)

WOMAN 1. (*ad lib*) If you knew time!

COMPANY.
IF YOU KNEW TIME

WOMAN 1. As well as I do!

COMPANY.
AS WELL AS I DO,

WOMAN 1. You'd never talk about wasting him!

COMPANY.
YOU'D NEVER TALK ABOUT WASTING HIM.

WOMAN 1. He never talks about wasting you!
COMPANY.
HE NEVER TALKS ABOUT WASTING YOU.
  WOMAN 1. (*sings*)
HE DOESN'T TALK,
HE DOESN'T TALK,
HE DOESN'T TALK.
(*ad lib*) If you knew time!
  COMPANY.
IF YOU KNEW TIME
  WOMAN 1. As well as I do!
  COMPANY.
AS WELL AS I DO,
  WOMAN 1. You'd never think about losing him!
  COMPANY.
YOU'D NEVER THINK ABOUT LOSING HIM.
  WOMAN 1. He never thinks about losing you!
  COMPANY.
HE NEVER THINKS ABOUT LOSING YOU.
  WOMAN 1. (*sings*)
HE DOESN'T THINK,
HE DOESN'T THINK,
HE DOESN'T THINK.
  COMPANY.
IF YOU KNEW TIME
AS WELL AS ME,
YOU WOULD KNOW THAT TIME HAS A
RIGHT TO BE FREE AND TIME SHOULD GO
ON, AND ON, AND ON.
IF YOU KNEW TIME
AS WELL AS I DO,
YOU'D NEVER THINK ABOUT KILLING HIM.
HE'S A VERY PEACEFUL SOUL
AND HE'D NEVER KILL YOU.
NO, HE'D NEVER KILL YOU.

[MUSIC NO. 15: NO ROOM — THE TEA PARTY]

(*Drum roll.*)

WOMAN 1. (*through megaphone*) Tea time! Ladies and
gentlemen, it gives us great pleasure to introduce to you the Mad

Hatter (*He enters and bows.*), the March Hare (*He enters and bows.*), the Dormouse (*He enters and bows.*), and their amazing tea table!

(*The TEA TABLE enters as the music vamps. The table consists of a large table top carried on the back of a cast member. On the table is a tablecloth that drapes all the way to the floor so that the audience cannot see the actor underneath. Glued to the top of the cloth are various cups and saucers. Throughout the following number the table moves back and forth and is followed by the characters.*)

HATTER.
NO ROOM, NO ROOM.
 ALICE.
THERE'S PLENTY OF ROOM.
 HATTER.
HAVE SOME WINE.
 ALICE.
I DON'T SEE ANY WINE.
 HATTER.
THERE ISN'T ANY.
 ALICE.
THEN IT WASN'T VERY CIVIL OF YOU TO OFFER IT.
 COMPANY.
IT WASN'T VERY CIVIL OF YOU TO SIT DOWN
WITHOUT BEING INVITED.
 ALICE.
I DIDN'T KNOW IT WAS YOUR TABLE.
IT'S LAID OUT FOR
A GREAT MANY MORE THAN THREE.
 HATTER.
YOU HAIR WANTS CUTTING.
 ALICE.
YOU SHOULD LEARN
NOT TO MAKE PERSONAL REMARKS,
IT'S VERY RUDE.
 HARE.
WHY IS A RAVEN LIKE A
WRITING DESK?
 ALICE.
OH, I LOVE RIDDLES,

I BELIEVE I CAN GUESS THAT.
> HATTER.

DO YOU MEAN THAT YOU THINK
YOU CAN FIND OUT THE ANSWER TO IT?
> ALICE. (*speaks*) Exactly so.

> HARE.

THEN YOU SHOULD SAY WHAT YOU MEAN.
> ALICE.

I DO, I MEAN WHAT I SAY.
IT'S THE SAME THING, YOU KNOW.
> HARE.

NOT THE SAME THING A BIT.
> COMPANY.

WHY YOU MIGHT JUST AS WELL SAY
THAT I SEE WHAT I EAT
IS THE SAME AS I EAT WHAT I SEE.
YOU MIGHT AS WELL SAY
THAT I LIKE WHAT I GET
IS THE SAME AS I GET WHAT I LIKE!
> DORMOUSE.

YOU MIGHT AS WELL SAY
THAT I BREATHE WHEN I SLEEP
IS THE SAME AS I SLEEP WHEN I BREATHE.
> COMPANY.

IT IS THE SAME THING WITH YOU.
> HATTER.

WHAT DAY OF THE MONTH IS IT?
> ALICE.

TUESDAY. (or name any other weekday)
> HATTER.

TWO DAYS WRONG!
I TOLD YOU BUTTER WOULDN'T SUIT THE WORKS.
> HARE. (*speaks*)

It was the best butter.
The Dormouse is asleep again.
> DORMOUSE. (*speaks*)

Of course, of course.
Just what I was going to remark myself.
> HATTER.

HAVE YOU GUESSED THE RIDDLE YET?
> ALICE.

NO, I GIVE UP.
WHAT IS THE ANSWER?

HATTER.
I HAVEN'T THE SLIGHTEST IDEA.
   HARE. (*speaks*)
Nor I.
   COMPANY.
NOR I.
   ALICE.
I THINK YOU MIGHT DO
SOMETHING BETTER WITH YOUR TIME
THAN WASTING IT IN RIDDLES
THAT HAVE NO ANSWERS.
   COMPANY.
IF YOU KNEW TIME
AS WELL AS IT DO,
YOU WOULDN'T TALK ABOUT
WASTING IT.
   HATTER. (*speaks*) It's him.
   COMPANY.
HE NEVER TALKS ABOUT WASTING YOU.
   ALICE.
YOU ALREADY TOLD ME THIS BEFORE, YOU KNOW.
   COMPANY.
OH, DORMOUSE, TELL US A STORY!
   ALICE.
YES, PLEASE DO DORMOUSE.
   COMPANY.
AND BE QUICK ABOUT IT
OR YOU'LL FALL ASLEEP AGAIN.
   DORMOUSE.
ONCE UPON A TIME THERE WERE THREE LITTLE
   SISTERS
AND THEIR NAMES WERE LACIE, TILLIE AND ELSIE,
AND THEY LIVED AT THE BOTTOM OF A WELL.
   ALICE.
WHAT DID THEY LIVE ON?
   DORMOUSE.
THEY LIVED ON TREACLE.
   ALICE.
THEY COULDN'T HAVE DONE THAT, YOU KNOW.
THEY'D HAVE BEEN ILL.
   DORMOUSE. (*speaks*)
They were, very ill!

COMPANY.
DOO BE DO BE DOO
DOO BE DO BE DOO
DOO BE DO BE DOO
DOO, DOO, DOO.

ALICE.
WHY DID THEY LIVE AT THE BOTTOM OF A WELL?

COMPANY.
DOO BE DO BE DOO
DOO BE DO BE DOO
DOO BE DO BE DOO
DOO, DOO, DOO.

HATTER. (*speaks*)
Have some more tea!

COMPANY.
DOO BE DO BE DOO
DOO BE DO BE DOO
DOO BE DO BE DOO
DOO, DOO, DOO.

ALICE. (*speaks*)
I've had nothing yet,
So how can I have more?

COMPANY.
DOO BE DO BE DOO
DOO BE DO BE DOO
DOO BE DO BE DOO
DOO, DOO, DOO.

HARE. (*speaks*)
You mean you can't take less.
It's very easy to take more than nothing.

COMPANY.
DOO BE DO BE DOO
DOO BE DO BE DOO
DOO BE DO BE DOO
DOO, DOO, DOO.

ALICE.
WHY DID THEY LIVE AT THE BOTTOM OF A WELL?

COMPANY.
DOO BE DO BE DOO
DOO BE DO BE DOO
DOO BE DO BE DOO
DOO, DOO, DOO

HATTER. (*speaks*)
It was a treacle well.
COMPANY.
DOO BE DO BE DOO
DOO BE DO BE DOO
DOO BE DO BE DOO
DOO, DOO, DOO
ALICE. (*speaks*)
There's no such thing!
COMPANY.
DOO BE DO BE DOO
DOO BE DO BE DOO
DOO BE DO BE DOO
DOO, DOO, DOO
DORMOUSE. Now these three little sisters . . . They were learning to draw, you know . . .
ALICE. What did they draw?

(*DORMOUSE, HATTER and HARE square off for an old-fashioned Western shoot-out. Drum roll.*)

DORMOUSE. Draw!

(*They fake drawing guns and shooting. All three fall down wounded and groaning.*)

COMPANY.
OH, DORMOUSE, TELL US A STORY.
ALICE.
YES, PLEASE DO, DORMOUSE.
COMPANY.
AND BE QUICK ABOUT IT
OR YOU'LL FALL ASLEEP AGAIN.

[MUSIC NO. 16: LEARNING TO DRAW]

(*ALICE starts to draw huge patterns with chalk on the stage floor. The COMPANY wanders slowly around watching her.*)

ALICE.
THEY WERE LEARNING TO DRAW . . .

COMPANY.
AND THEY DREW
ALL MANNER OF THINGS.
EVERYTHING
THAT BEGINS
WITH AN "M"
SUCH AS MOUSETRAPS
AND THE MOON . . .
AND MEMORY . . .
AND MUCHNESS.
YOU KNOW YOU SAY
THINGS ARE MUCH
OF A MUCHNESS.

DID YOU EVER
SEE SUCH A THING
AS A DRAWING
DRAWING OF A
MUCHNESS?

ALICE.
AND THEY DREW
ALL MANNER OF THINGS.
EVERYTHING
THAT BEGINS
WITH AN "M"
MOUSETRAPS
AND MOON . . .
AND MEMORY . . .
AND MUCHNESS . . .

YOU SAY THINGS
ARE MUCH OF A
MUCHNESS.
NO I NEVER
SAW A
DRAWING OF A
MUCHNESS.

[MUSIC NO. 17: STARTING OUT AGAIN]

(*ALICE starts to wipe out the chalk with her foot, and this
action turns into a soft shoe tap dance as the music begins.*)

ALICE.
STARTING OUT AGAIN
MAKING UP FOR LOST TIME.
WISHING THERE WAS
SOMETHING MORE THAN THIS,
BUT THERE'S NOT SO I AM
    COMPANY.
STARTING OUT AGAIN
    ALICE.
IT'S ALWAYS TEATIME.
    COMPANY.
MAKING UP FOR LOST
    TIME.
WISHING THERE WAS
SOMETHING MORE THAN
    THIS,
BUT THERE'S

ALICE.
YOU KNOW IT'S TEA-
    TIME.

NO MATTER HOW IT
    TICKETY TOCKS
IT'S ALWAYS TEATIME

NOT SO I AM   ON OUR CLOCKS
STARTING OUT AGAIN
    ALICE & COMPANY.
CHANGING THE RULES OF THE GAME
    COMPANY.   ALICE.
WE'RE GONNA PAINT THE   SURELY
RED QUEEN'S   I WILL
CROQUET GARDEN,   BREAK THEM
    WE'RE
GONNA PAINT THE   FAST AS
RED QUEEN'S   I CAN
CROQUET GARDEN   MAKE THEM
THAT'S   THAT'S
A PART OF IT, TOO,   A PART OF IT, TOO,
WHEN YOU KEEP   WHEN YOU KEEP
THE RED   STARTING OUT AGAIN
QUEEN   MAKING UP FOR
MAKES   LOST TIME
US   WISHING THERE WAS
SO   SOMETHING MORE THAN
SCARED,   THIS,
WE'RE   BUT THERE'S
RUNNING, RUNNING,   NOT SO
RUNNING, RUNNING   I AM
    TRIO. (Men 1, 2, & 3)
THE RED   STARTING OUT AGAIN
QUEEN   MAKING UP FOR
MAKES   LOST TIME
US   WISHING THERE WAS
SO   SOMETHING MORE THAN
SCARED   THIS
THAT WE ARE . . .

[MUSIC NO. 18: WHITE ROSES RED]

(*The TRIO—MEN 1, 2, & 3— is huddled together at one side
of the stage. The RED QUEEN is offstage, but ducks her
head out each time she has a line.*)

    TRIO.
. . . PAINTING THE WHITE ROSES RED.

QUEEN.
AHHHHHHHHH.
   MAN 3. It's the Red Queen!
   TRIO.
WE ARE TRYING TO KEEP OUR DEAR HEADS.
   QUEEN.
AHHHHHHHHH.
   ALICE. She sounds viscious.
   TRIO.
WE ARE SO FOND OF OUR HEADS.
   QUEEN.
AHHHHHHHHH.
   ALICE. A savage soprano.
   TRIO.
WE WOULD NOT LIKE TO BE DEAD!
   QUEEN.
AHHHHHHHHH.
   ALICE. Keep your voices down.
   TRIO.
SO WE ARE PAINTING . . .
   QUEEN.
AHHHHHHH.
   TRIO.
THE WHITE RO . . .
   QUEEN.
AHHHHHH.
   TRIO.
'SES RED.

[MUSIC NO. 19: DIALOGUE BEFORE THE ALPHABET]

*(ALICE gets down on the floor and starts writing big letters
   of the alphabet as she sings them.)*

   ALICE.
A . . . B . . . C . . .
   COMPANY. *(ad lib)* Miss, you can't do that. *(Etc.; they try to
erase what she has written.)*

*(The RED QUEEN enters and approaches ALICE, who con-
   tinues to sing and write.)*

ALICE.

. . . D, E, F, G, H, I, J, K, L, M, N, O, P, Q . . .

QUEEN. Who are you?

ALICE. I am Alice Pleasance Liddell, so please Your Majesty.

QUEEN. Oh, Alice Pleasance Liddell! What are you doing?

ALICE. I am doing the alphabet, so please Your Majesty.

QUEEN. Well! If you really want to please my Majesty . . .
(*She screams.*) . . . *don't do the alphabet, just say the letter Q!!*

[MUSIC NO. 20: THE ALPHABET]

(*A TRIO—WOMAN 1, MAN 2 & MAN 5—perform a dance,
intertwining with other COMPANY members and acting
out the lines of the song as they sing. The QUEEN watches
with pleasure.*)

COMPANY.

DON'T DO THE ALPHABET,
JUST SAY THE LETTER Q.

WOMAN 1.	COMPANY.
A WAS ONCE AN APPLIE PIE	SHOO A-DEE-A, SHOO A-DEE-A
PIDY, WIDY, TIDY, PIDY	SHOO A-DEE-A,
NICE INSIDY APPLE PIE.	SHOO A-DEE-A.

COMPANY.

DON'T DO THE ALPHABET,
JUST SAY THE LETTER Q.

MAN. 2.	COMPANY.
B WAS ONCE A LITTLE BEAR,	SHOO B-DEE-B, SHOO B-DEE-B
BEARY, WARY, HAIRY, TARY	SHOO B-DEE-B,
CARY LITTLE BEAR.	SHOO B-DEE-B.

COMPANY.

DON'T DO THE ALPHABET,
JUST SAY THE LETTER Q.

MAN 5.
C WAS A CAT, WHO RAN
    AFTER A RAT
BUT HIS COURAGE DID
    FAIL
WHEN SHE SEIZED ON
    HIS TAIL.
    TRIO.
C! CRAFTY OLD CAT!

COMPANY.
C-C-DEE DEE, C-C-DEE
    DEE,
C-C-DEE DEE,

C-C-DEE DEE.

COMPANY.
DON'T DO THE ALPHABET,
JUST SAY THE LETTER Q.

D WAS A DUCK WITH SPOTS ON HIS BACK.

TRIO.
WHO LIVED IN THE WATER
AND ALWAYS SAID QUACK!
    COMPANY.
QUACK!
DON'T DO THE ALPHABET
JUST SAY THE LETTER Q.

TRIO.
E WAS AN ELEPHANT,
STATELY AND WISE;
HE HAD TWO LITTLE TUSKS
AND TWO QUEER LITTLE EYES.

COMPANY.
DON'T DO THE ALPHABET,
JUST SAY THE LETTER Q.

TRIO.
F WAS A FISH
WHO WAS CAUGHT IN A NET,
BUT HE GOT OUT AGAIN,
AND IS QUITE ALIVE YET.

COMPANY.
DON'T DO THE ALPHABET,
JUST SAY THE LETTER Q.

G WAS PAPA'S NEW GUN
  TRIO.
DON'T DO THE ALPHABET.
  COMPANY.
HE PUT IT IN A BOX.
  TRIO.
JUST SAY THE LETTER Q.
  COMPANY.
THEN HE WENT AND BOUGHT A BUN:
  TRIO. (*spoken*) Don't do the alphabet.
  COMPANY.
AND WALKED ABOUT THE DOCKS.

(*By this time COMPANY is seated in a row along the platform.*)

DON'T DO THE ALPHABET,
JUST SAY THE LETTER Q.
DON'T DO THE ALPHABET,
JUST SAY THE LETTER Q.
  MAN 1. (*stands up*) Queen! (*sits down*)
  COMPANY.
DON'T DO THE ALPHABET,
JUST SAY THE LETTER Q.
  WOMAN 1. (*stands up*) Red . . . (*sits down*)
  MAN 1. (*stands up*) Queen. (*sits down*)
  COMPANY.
DON'T DO THE ALPHABET,
JUST SAY THE LETTER Q.
  MAN 3. (*stands up*) Her majesty the . . . (*sits down*)
  WOMAN 1. (*stands up*) Red . . . (*sits down*)
  MAN 1. (*stands up*) Queen. (*sits down*)
  COMPANY.
DON'T DO THE ALPHABET,
JUST SAY THE LETTER Q.
  MAN 5. (*stands up*) Her highest . . . (*sits down*)
  MAN 3. (*stands up*) Majesty the . . . (*sits down*)
  WOMAN 1. (*stands up*) Red . . . (*sits down*)
  MAN 1. (*stands up*) Queen. (*sits down*)
  COMPANY.
DON'T DO THE ALPHABET,
JUST SAY THE LETTER Q.
  MAN 2. (*stands up*) Or she'll behead you! (*sits down*)
  MAN 5. (*stands up*) Her highest . . . (*sits down*)

MAN 3. (*stands up*) Majesty the . . . (*sits down*)
WOMAN 1. (*stands up*) Red . . . (*sits down*)
MAN 1. (*stands up*) Queen. (*sits down*)
COMPANY.
DON'T DO THE ALPHABET,
JUST SAY THE LETTER Q.
WOMAN 4. (*stands up*) Here she comes! (*sits down*)
COMPANY. Oh no!
QUEEN. (*chants*)
Off with her head.
Off with her head.
Off with her head,
Off with her head.

[MUSIC NO. 21: THE RED QUEEN]

(*During this number the QUEEN struts about threatening the MEN in the company who hover around her to do her bidding.*)

QUEEN.
I SAY DON'T LOOK FOR
ANOTHER SOLUTION,
OFF WITH THEIR HEADS!
MEN.
OFF WITH THEIR HEADS!
QUEEN.
WHAT IS THIS STUFF OF
FORGIVE AND FORGET IT?
OFF WITH THEIR HEADS!
MEN.
OFF WITH THEIR HEADS!

QUEEN.	MEN.
OTHERS MAY TRY TO	AH
GIVE THE APPEARANCE	AH
OF BEING FAIR,	AH
THEY'RE JUST SCARED . . .	AH,
	THEY'RE JUST SCARED.
WOULDN'T THEY LOVE TO	AH
HAVE ONE ON THEIR	AH
MANTLES	

AS MANY HEADS AS ME   AH
THEY WOULDN'T DARE . . .   AH,
                                    THEY WOULDN'T
                                      DARE
                                    THEY WOULDN'T
                                      DARE
                                    THEY WOULDN'T
                                      DARE

I AM JUST DOING WHAT
COMES NATURALLY TO ME
CUTTING OFF HEADS.
   MEN.
CUTTING OFF HEADS.
   QUEEN.
YOU KNOW FOR YEARS IT'S BEEN
A POPULAR HOBBY
MAKING PEOPLE DEAD.
   MEN.
BETTER THAN DEAD!
   QUEEN.   MEN.
WHEN I MEET A PERSON WHO   AH
RUBS ME THE WRONG WAY   AH
I DON'T TAKE THE TIME TO   AH
  WONDER
WHY . . .   AH,
                                   WHY WONDER?

WHY WASTE A MOMENT ON   AH
SLAVES WHO DON'T ADORE   AH
  ME,
JUST CUT OFF THEIR HEADS   AH
AND WATCH THEM DIE . . .   AH,
                                   AND WATCH THEM
                                     DIE,
                                   WATCH THEM DIE,
                                   WATCH THEM DIE.
YOU MAY THINK THAT
I'M AN OGRE,
I AM JUST THE
QUEEN-NEXT-DOOR I
SIMPLY HAVE AN AXE INSTEAD OF A
CUP OF SUGAR.

THAT IS NOTHING MUCH TO BE AFRAID OF
AS LONG AS YOU AGREE THAT
I AM ABSOLUTELY PERFECT.
    COMPANY.
YOU MAY THINK
THAT SHE'S AN OGRE
SHE IS JUST THE
QUEEN NEXT DOOR SHE SIMPLY
HAS AN AXE INSTEAD OF A
CUP OF SUGAR.
THAT IS NOTHING MUCH TO BE AFRAID OF
AS LONG AS YOU AGREE THAT
SHE IS ABSOLUTELY PERFECT.
    QUEEN & COMPANY.
OFF WITH HER HEAD!
OFF WITH HER HEAD!
OFF WITH HER HEAD!
OFF WITH HER HEAD!
AH, AH

(*The QUEEN approaches ALICE at center stage. The QUEEN then calls to the flamingo, a large stuffed toy located in the balcony or offstage.*)

    QUEEN. (*calling to flamingo*) Come on, baby, Jump.
    ALICE. This is the most curious croquet-ground I've ever seen.
    QUEEN. Isn't it lovely?
    ALICE. It's all ridges and furrows. The croquet balls are live hedgehogs, and the mallets are live flamingos.
    FLAMINGO. Ahhhhhhhh! (*It is thrown from balcony and lands on stage at ALICE's feet. At the director's option, anyone can scream as the flamingo.*)
    ALICE. (*picks up flamingo and attempts to demonstrate playing croquet with it as she speaks*) The chief difficulty seems to be managing the flamingo. Just as you get its body tucked away, comfortably enough under your arm, with it's legs hanging down, and just as you get it's neck nicely straightened out, and are going to give the hedgehog a blow with its head, it looks up in your face with such a puzzled expression that you burst out laughing. (*COMPANY laughs.*) I've come to the conclusion that it is a very difficult game indeed.

[MUSIC NO. 22: NEVER PLAY CROQUET]

(*This song is chanted in rhythm, in imitation of Bob Dylan's sing-songy non-melodic style, i.e. "Like a Rolling Stone."*)

MAN 3.
NEVER PLAY CROQUET WITH A
BALL THAT'S A HEDGEHOG 'CAUSE THE
HEDGEHOG WILL RUN AWAY.

NEVER HIT A HEDGEHOG WITH
THE BEAK OF A FLAMINGO 'CAUSE
THAT'S NOT HOW TO PLAY CROQUET.

AND YOU'LL BE STUCK
WITH YOUR PUCK
IN THE MUCK
AND YOU'LL BE STUCK
(*spoken*) Help me everybody.
    COMPANY.
AND YOU'LL BE STUCK
WITH YOUR PUCK
IN THE MUCK
AND YOU'LL BE STUCK.
    WOMAN 4.
NEVER PLAY CROQUET WITH A
BALL THAT'S A HEDGEHOG 'CAUSE THE
HEDGEHOG WILL RUN AWAY.

NEVER HIT A HEDGEHOG WITH THE
BEAK OF A FLAMINGO, 'CAUSE
THAT'S NOT HOW TO PLAY CROQUET.

    MAN 1.
AND YOU'LL BE STUCK
WITH YOUR PUCK
IN THE MUCK
AND YOU'LL BE STUCK.
    COMPANY.
AND YOU'LL BE STUCK
WITH YOUR PUCK

IN THE MUCK
AND YOU'LL BE STUCK.

 ALICE. (*sings sweetly*)
I SEE LOTS OF HEDGEHOGS RUNNING
I SEE LOTS OF FLAMINGOS SUNNING
THEMSELVES IN THE TROPICAL AIR.
IT ISN'T FAIR.

 COMPANY.
IT'S MY TURN NOW.

NEVER PLAY CROQUET WITH A
BALL THAT'S A HEDGEHOG, 'CAUSE
THE HEDGEHOG WILL RUN AWAY.

 COMPANY.
NEVER HIT A HEDGEHOG WITH THE
BEAK OF A FLAMINGO, 'CAUSE
THAT'S NOT HOW TO PLAY
CROQUET.
AND YOU'LL BE STUCK
WITH YOUR PUCK
IN THE MUCK
AND YOU'LL BE STUCK.

AND YOU'LL BE STUCK
WITH YOUR PUCK
IN THE MUCK
AND YOU'LL BE STUCK.

AND YOU'LL BE STUCK
WITH YOUR PUCK
IN THE MUCK
AND YOU'LL BE . . .

 ALICE. I don't think they play at all fairly.

 COMPANY.
STUCK!

[MUSIC NO. 23: THE MOCK TURTLE'S STORY]

(*Sad soupy violin music begins. ALICE approaches MOCK
TURTLE and GRYPHON who are seated at a small kitchen
table. TURTLE is sobbing. He is a sad old man who moans
and whines about everything. GRYPHON is a woman who
is fed up with his griping.*)

ALICE. (*to GRYPHON*) What's his sorrow?

GRYPHON. He hasn't got any sorrow. It's all his fancy. Shhhh. There's a girl here who wants to hear your story. She does.

TURTLE. I'll tell her. *Quiet*, both of you, 'til I've finished my story. (*He sobs.*)

ALICE. I don't see how he can ever finish, if he doesn't begin.

TURTLE. Once, I was a real Turtle. (*Violin gets soupier and soupier.*) When we were little, we went to school under the sea. The master was an old turtle. We used to call him Tortoise.

ALICE. Why did you call him Tortoise if he wasn't one?

TURTLE. We called him Tortoise because he taught us. (*COM-PANY laughs.*) Really, you are very dull!

GRYPHON. You ought to be ashamed of yourself for asking such a stupid question.

TURTLE. We went to school in the sea, though you mayn't believe it.

ALICE. I never said I didn't!

TURTLE. You did!

GRYPHON. Hold your tongue!

TURTLE. She did, I heard her! We had the best of educations. We went to school every day.

ALICE. I go to school every day too. You needn't be so proud as all that.

TURTLE. With extras?

ALICE. Yes, with French and music.

TURTLE. And washing?

ALICE. Washing? Certainly not.

TURTLE. Ah! Then yours wasn't a really good school. Now at ours, they had, at the end of the bill, French, music and washing — extra!

ALICE. You couldn't have wanted it much, living at the bottom of the sea.

TURTLE. Ahhhhh! (*Sobbing; the violin increases in volume.*)

GRYPHON. Enough with the violin, already! (*The violin stops. TURTLE gestures, and the violin begins again*).

TURTLE. I couldn't afford to learn it. I only took the regular course.

ALICE. What was that?

TURTLE. Oh, you know. Reeling and Writhing, of course, to begin with, and then the different branches of Arithmetic — Ambition, Distraction, Uglification and Derision.

ALICE. Thank you very much for your story. (*She starts to leave; the violin stops.*)

TURTLE. Wait a minute. Remember, a wise fish never goes anywhere without a porpoise.

ALICE. What?

TURTLE. When a young fish comes to me and says he is going on a journey, I say "With what porpoise?"

ALICE. OK. (*She starts to leave again.*)

TURTLE. Wait. Have you ever heard of the Lobster Quadrille? (*GRYPHON gestures "Yes!" behind TURTLE.*)

ALICE. No, what is it?

TURTLE. It's a dance. It's a dance we used to do under the sea. We have a boy here, he's going to sing it for you. Just a few bars. Keep it short.

[MUSIC NO. 24: THE LOBSTER QUADRILLE]

(*MAN 5 stands to one side with a microphone. He croons the tune like a particularly bad Las Vegas nightclub singer with pauses and sexy poses. ALICE is sitting off to side. She watches him in a trance. He is her favorite matinee idol. After each line she swoons and shrieks.*)

MAN 5.
"WILL YOU WALK A LITTLE FASTER?"
SAID A WHITING TO A SNAIL.
"THERE'S A PORPOISE CLOSE BEHIND US,
AND HE'S TREADING ON MY TAIL.
SEE HOW EAGERLY THE LOBSTERS
AND THE TURTLES ALL ADVANCE.
THEY ARE WAITING ON THE SHINGLE.
WON'T . . . (*He searches audience, then spots ALICE and points at her.*)
YOU
(*She jumps up shrieking in ecstasy.*)
COME AND JOIN THE DANCE?"

(*ALICE goes to MAN 5 and they do a waltz during the following musical section. Rest of the COMPANY also select partners and dance.*)

COMPANY.	TURTLE. (*speaks over the*
WILL YOU,	*singing*) What a dance that
WON'T YOU,	was. Not like what these

WILL YOU,
WON'T YOU
WILL YOU,
WON'T YOU
JOIN THE DANCE?

young turtles do today. We'd
all line up, the seals, the turtles, the porpoises, and each
one with a lobster for a
partner.

(*WOMAN 1 grabs microphone and steps up on platform to sing.
She has everyone's attention including TURTLE who walks
over to her and stares at her in adoring amazement, a slight
gleam in his senile old eyes.*)

WOMAN 1. (*sings in very sultry, jazz-like nightclub style*)
"YOU CAN REALLY HAVE NO NOTION
HOW DELIGHTFUL IT WILL BE
WHEN THEY TAKE US UP AND THROW US
WITH THE LOBSTERS OUT TO SEA."
BUT THE SNAIL REPLIED "TOO FAR,
TOO FAR" AND GAVE A LOOK ASKANCE.
SAID HE THANKED THE WHITING KINDLY,
BUT HE WOULD NOT JOIN,
HE WOULD NOT JOIN
(*She starts to groove on phrase and scats the next few lines.
TURTLE gets even closer.*)
HE WOULD NOT JOIN,
HE WOULD NOT JOIN
HE WOULD NOT JOIN
  TURTLE. (*tries to imitate her into microphone*)
HE WOULD NOT JOIN.
  WOMAN 1.
HE WOULD NOT JOIN.
  TURTLE.
HE . . . (*chokes*)
  WOMAN 1.
HE WOULD NOT JOIN THE,
HE WOULD NOT JOIN THE,
HE WOULD NOT JOIN THE,
HE WOULD NOT JOIN THE,
WHOOOOO!
DANCE.

(*The COMPANY begins waltzing again.*)

COMPANY.
WOULD NOT,
COULD NOT,
WOULD NOT,
COULD NOT,
WOULD NOT,
COULD NOT,
JOIN THE DANCE.

TURTLE. (*speaks over singing*) One step forward, everyone change lobsters, then one step back, pick up your lobster, twirl it around your head, and throw it as far as you can out to sea. And as they swam back, we did a little step on the shore. (*Speech should be timed to finish before music does.*)

MAN 1.
"WHAT MATTERS HOW FAR WE GO?"
HIS SCALY FRIEND REPLIED.
WOMAN 3.
"THERE IS ANOTHER SHORE, YOU KNOW
UPON THE OTHER SIDE."
QUARTET. (*MAN 1 & 5, WOMAN 1 & 3*) (*a capella*)
THE FURTHER OFF FROM ENGLAND
THE NEARER IS TO FRANCE.
TURTLE.
THEN TURN NOT PALE, BELOVED SNAIL,
BUT COME AND JOIN THE DANCE.
ALICE.
WILL YOU, WON'T YOU.
WILL YOU, WON'T YOU.
ALICE & COMPANY.
WILL YOU, WON'T YOU
JOIN THE DANCE?

[MUSIC NO. 25: EATING MUSHROOMS]

(*COMPANY and ALICE spread out around the performance area and wander slowly around the stage looking all around as if lost.*)

ALICE.
EATING MUSHROOMS.
COMPANY.
EATING MUSHROOMS.
ALICE.
DRINKING DRINKS.

COMPANY.
DRINKING DRINKS.
ALICE.
STARTING SMALLER.
COMPANY.
STARTING SMALLER.
ALICE.
GROWING BIGGER.
COMPANY.
GROWING BIGGER.
ALICE.
CHANGING WORLDS.
COMPANY.
CHANGING WORLDS.
ALICE.
FAST AS YOU CAN THINK.
COMPANY.
FAST AS YOU CAN THINK.
ALICE.
MEETING CREATURES.
COMPANY.
MEETING CREATURES.
ALICE.
MAD AS HATTERS.
COMPANY.
MAD AS HATTERS.
ALICE.
COLORS CHANGING.
COMPANY.
COLORS CHANGING.
ALICE.
WORLDS REARRANGING.
COMPANY.
WORLDS REARRANGING.
ALICE.
I HAVE NEVER BEEN IN SUCH A
STATE BEFORE.
COMPANY.
YOU HAVE NEVER BEEN IN SUCH A
STATE BEFORE.
ALICE.
NEVER BEEN IN WONDER-
LAND BEFORE.

COMPANY.
NEVER BEEN IN WONDER-
LAND BEFORE.
ALICE.
I SUPPOSE THIS IS
A REGULAR DAY
IF YOU'RE MAD.
COMPANY.
I SUPPOSE THIS IS
A REGULAR DAY
IF YOU'RE MAD.
ALICE & COMPANY.
CURIOSER AND CURIOSER AND
CURIOSER AND CURIOSER.

(*The following is a round started by ALICE and picked up by rest of COMPANY.*)

CATS HALF HERE AND CATS HALF NOT.
MOUSES DRINKING TEA WITH NO TEA IN THEIR POTS.
MOMMIES BEATING BABIES AND BABIES THAT SNORT.
ONE TIME I'M ENORMOUS AND THE NEXT TIME
  SHORT.
I'M SHORT. I'M SHORT.

COMPANY.
YOU HAVE NEVER BEEN IN SUCH A
STATE BEFORE.
ALICE.
NEVER BEEN IN WONDER-
LAND BEFORE.
COMPANY.
NEVER BEEN IN WONDER-
LAND BEFORE.
ALICE.
I SUPPOSE THIS IS
A REGULAR DAY IF YOU'RE
MAD.
COMPANY.
I SUPPOSE THIS IS
A REGULAR DAY IF YOU'RE
MAD.

ALICE & COMPANY.
CURIOSER AND CURIOSER AND
CURIOSER AND CURIOSER AND
CURIOSER AND CURIOSER AND . . .
OOOOOOOO . . .

(*Lights dim, then fade out.*)

End of ACT 1

ACT TWO

[MUSIC CUE NO. 26: CHILD OF PURE UNCLOUDED BROW]

(This number is sung a capella by WOMAN 1 and MAN 2. As lights come up they are seen standing on the platform. ALICE is seated on the floor in front of them playing with her cat. ALICE's speeches are timed to approximately begin and end with the verses of the song.)

ALICE. (*spoken*) Do you know what today is, Kitty? You'd have guessed if you were up in the window with me. I was watching the boys getting in stocks for the bonfire—it wants plenty of sticks, Kitty, only it got so cold, and it snowed so, they had to leave off. Never mind, Kitty, we'll go see the bonfire tomorrow.

WOMAN 1.
CHILD OF PURE UN-
    CLOUDED BROW,
AND DREAMING EYES OF
    WONDER!
THOUGH TIME BE FLEET
AND I AND THOU
ARE HALF A LIFE
    ASUNDER,
THY LOVING SMILE WILL
SURELY HAIL,
THE LOVE GIFT OF A
FAIRY-TALE!

ALICE. I'm saving up all your punishments for Wednesday next. Suppose they saved up all my punishments. What would they do at the end of a year? I should have to go without, fifty dinners at once! Well, I shouldn't mind that. I'd rather go without them than eat them.

WOMAN 1 & MAN 2.
A TALE BEGUN IN OTHER
    DAYS
WHEN SUMMER SUNS
    WERE GLOWING
A SIMPLE CHIME,
THAT SERVED TO TIME
    THE RHYTHM
OF OUR ROWING.
WHOSE ECHOES LIVE IN
    MEMORY YET,
THOUGH ENVIOUS YEARS
    WOULD SAY
'FORGET.'

ALICE. Hush, Kitty. Do you hear the snow against the windowpane? How nice and soft it sounds. Just as if

WOMAN 1 & MAN 2.
COME, HARKEN THEM,
    ERE
VOICE OF DREAD,
WITH BITTER TIDINGS

someone was kissing the window all over outside. I wonder if the snow loves the trees and the fields that it kisses them so gently? And then it covers them up snug, you know, with a white quilt: and perhaps it says, 'go to sleep, darlings, till the summer comes.'

ALICE. And when they wake up in the summer, Kitty, they dress themselves all in green and dance about —oh, that's very pretty! I wish it were true. I'm sure the woods look sleepy in autumn when the leaves are getting brown.

LADEN.
SHALL SUMMON TO UN-
   WELCOME BED
A MELANCHOLY MAIDEN!
WE ARE BUT OLDER
   CHILDREN,
DEAR,
WHO FRET TO FIND OUR
   BEDTIME
NEAR.
WOMAN 1 & MAN 2.
AND THOUGH THE
   SHADOW OF A SIGH
MAY TREMBLE THROUGH
   THE STORY,
FOR HAPPY SUMMER
   DAYS GONE BY,
AND VANISHED SUMMER
   GLORY—
IT SHALL NOT TOUCH
WITH BREATH OF BALE,
THE PLEASANCE OF OUR
   FAIRY TALE
THE PLEASANCE OF OUR
   FAIRY TALE.

[MUSIC NO. 27: JABBERWOCKY]

(*The COMPANY slowly appears onstage and sits on the platform. ALICE remains on the floor with Kitty during the following speech.*)

ALICE. Do you want to hear all my ideas about Looking Glass House, Kitty? It's very much like our house, only things go the other way. I know this, because if I hold a book up, they hold one up, too. Only all the words go the other way.

(*The JABBERWOCK [MAN 5] steathily approaches and circles her.*)

JABBERWOCK. (*sings raga-style*)
'TWAS BRILLIG—

ALICE. 'Twas brillig and the slithy toves . . .
JABBERWOCK.
AND THE SLITHY TOVES
ALICE. Did gyre . . .
JABBERWOCK.
DID GYRE
ALICE. . . . gimble.
JABBERWOCK.
AND GIMBLE IN THE WABE
ALICE. All mimsy were the borogoves.
JABBERWOCK.
ALL MIMSY WERE THE BOROGOVES,
ALICE. And the mome raths outgrabe.
JABBERWOCK.
AND THE MOME RATHS OUTGRABE.

'TWAS BRILLIG AND THE SLITHY TOVES
DID GYRE AND GIMBLE IN THE WABE:
ALL MIMSY WERE THE BOROGOVES,
AND THE MOME RATHS OUTGRABE.

COMPANY.
BEWARE THE JABBERWOCK, MY SON!
THE JAWS THAT BITE, THE CLAWS THAT CATCH!
BEWARE THE JUBJUB BIRD, AND SHUN
THE FRUMIOUS BANDERSNATCH!

MAN 3.
HE TOOK HIS VORPAL SWORD IN HAND;
LONG TIME THE MANXOME FOE HE SOUGHT
SO RESTED HE BY THE TUMTUM TREE,
AND STOOD AWHILE IN THOUGHT.

COMPANY.
BEWARE THE JABBERWOCK, MY SON!
THE JAWS THAT BITE, THE CLAWS THAT CATCH!
BEWARE THE JUBJUB BIRD, AND SHUN
THE FRUMIOUS BANDERSNATCH!

MAN 4.
AND AS AN UFFISH THOUGHT HE STOOD,
THE JABBERWOCK, WITH EYES OF FLAME,

CAME WIFFLING THROUGH THE TULGEY WOOD,
AND BURBLED AS IT CAME!
ALICE. Look out!

COMPANY.
BEWARE THE JABBERWOCK, MY SON!
THE JAWS THAT BITE, THE CLAWS THAT CATCH!
BEWARE THE JUBJUB BIRD, AND SHUN
THE FRUMIOUS BANDERSNATCH!

MAN 2.
ONE, TWO! ONE, TWO! AND THROUGH AND THROUGH
THE VORPAL BLADE WENT SNICKER-SNACK!
HE LEFT IT DEAD, AND WITH ITS HEAD
HE WENT GALUMPHING BACK.
COMPANY.
BEWARE THE JABBERWOCK, MY SON!
THE JAWS THAT BITE, THE CLAWS THAT CATCH!
BEWARE THE JUBJUB BIRD, AND SHUN
THE FRUMIOUS BANDERSNATCH!

(*JABBERWOCKY FIGHT: ALICE has a fight with the JAB-
BERWOCK, accompanied in the orchestra by a 24-bar
rhythm section. ALICE and the JABBERWOCK both have
large sticks and they spar with them as they circle one
another. The 24-bar section is repeated four times, and the
character of the fight can change with each repeat. During
the last 24-bar section ALICE slays the JABBERWOCK,
and then drops to her knees by his side and sobs.*)

COMPANY.
HAST THOU SLAIN THE JABBERWOCK?
COME TO MY ARMS, MY BEAMISH BOY.
OH, FRABJOUS DAY! CALOO! CALLAY!
ALICE.
HE CHORTED IN HIS JOY.

COMPANY.	COMPANY. (*counter melody*)
BEWARE	OH, HE'S A MONSTER
THE JABBERWOCK,	OH YES,
MY SON!	YOU'D BETTER
THE JAWS THAT BITE,	GET AWAY

THE CLAWS THAT CATCH!
BEWARE
THE JUBJUB BIRD, AND SHUN
THE FRUMIOUS BANDERSNATCH!
FROM THAT MONSTER JABBERWOCK
YOU'D BETTER GET AWAY
FROM THAT MONSTER JABBERWOCK!

COMPANY.
'TWAS BRILLIG AND THE SLITHY TOVES
DID GYRE AND GIMBLE IN THE WABE:
ALL MIMSY WERE THE BOROGOVES,
AND THE MOME RATHS OUTGRABE.
AND THE MOME RATHS OUTGRABE.
AND THE MOME RATHS OUTGRABE.

(*JABBERWOCK gets up and slowly retreats. ALICE remains seated, legs crossed at center stage. COMPANY begins to arrange itself behind her in a semicircle, chanting the following:*)

COMPANY. (*chanting*)
Humpty Dumpty sat on a wall.
Humpty Dumpty had a great fall.
All the King's horses and all the King's men
Couldn't put Humpty together again.

Humpty Dumpty sat on a wall.
Humpty Dumpty had a great fall.
All the King's horses and all the King's men
Couldn't put Humpty together again.

[MUSIC NO. 28: HUMPTY DUMPTY]

(*ALICE becomes HUMPTY DUMPTY, singing the following song as a fat, pompous old man with a hollow, deep voice. She remains seated with her legs crossed and her arms wrapped around them, rolling from side to side on her behind.*)

HUMPTY-DUMPTY. (*part singing and spoken*)
IT'S VERY PROVOKING

TO BE CALLED AN EGG. VERY.
SOME PEOPLE HAVE NO MORE SENSE THAN A BABY.
SOME PEOPLE HAVE NO MORE SENSE THAN A BABY.

WHY DO I SIT HERE ALL ALONE?
Because there's no one with me.
WHY DO I SIT HERE ALL ALONE?
Because there's no one with me
DID YOU THINK I DIDN'T KNOW THE
ANSWER TO THAT? Ask another.
DID YOU THINK I DIDN'T KNOW THE
ANSWER TO THAT? Ask another.

WHY AREN'T I SAFER ON THE GROUND
IF THIS WALL IS SO VERY NARROW?
You may ask me
WHY AREN'T I SAFER ON THE GROUND
If this wall is so very narrow.

WHY, IF I EVER DID FALL OFF
Which there's no chance of.
Which there's no chance of.
THE KING HAS PROMISED ME . . .
Ah, you turn pale, you didn't think I was going to say that, did
you?
THE KING HAS PROMISED ME
With his very own mouth
To . . . To . . . To . . .
　　COMPANY.
TO SEND ALL HIS HORSES
AND ALL HIS MEN
　　HUMPTY-DUMPTY.
YES SEND ALL HIS HORSES
AND ALL HIS MEN.

[MUSIC NO. 29: HUMPTY DUMPTY CHORALE]

(*The COMPANY stands up formally; ALICE remains seated
in front of them.*)

　　COMPANY.
WHEN SOMEONE TELLS ME
I WILL BE THERE

I'M NOT SUSPICIOUS,
I REALLY CARE.
WHEN SOMEONE SAYS HE'LL HELP ME
I BELIEVE HIM.
THIS IS SIMPLE LOGIC.
  HUMPTY-DUMPTY. (*groaning*) Ohhhhhhhhhh!
  COMPANY.
NOT HARD TO DO
  HUMPTY-DUMPTY. Oh my God!
  COMPANY.
VERY SIMPLE LOGIC.
  HUMPTY-DUMPTY. Shhpshhspshhh!
  COMPANY.
ONE AND ONE IS TWO.

(*The COMPANY returns to the platform and sits. ALICE gets
    up and wanders around.*)

  ALICE. I wonder which of these signposts leads out of the
woods.

[MUSIC NO. 30: TWEEDLEDUM AND TWEEDLEDEE]

(*TWEEDLEDUM and TWEEDLEDEE stand to one side. When
    they start to sing ALICE turns and walks over to them.*)

  TWEEDLEDUM & TWEEDLEDEE.
IF YOU THINK WE'RE WAX-WORKS
YOU OUGHT TO PAY, YOU KNOW.
WAX WORKS WEREN'T MADE TO BE LOOKED AT
FOR NOTHIN', NO HOW.
CONTRARIWISE,
IF YOU THINK WE'RE ALIVE,
YOU OUGHT TO SPEAK.
  ALICE.
I'M SURE I'M VERY SORRY

(*TWEEDLEDUM and TWEEDLEDEE begin to fight, flailing
    their arms at each other and reciting the following:*)

  TWEEDLEDUM & TWEEDLEDEE.
Tweedledum and Tweedledee

Agreed to have a battle.
For Tweedledum said Tweedledee
Had spoiled his nice new rattle.

Just then flew down a monstrous crow,
As black as a tar barrel;
Which frightened both our heroes so
They quite forgot their quarrel.

(*TWEEDLEDUM falls asleep standing up.*)

TWEEDLEDEE. Isn't he a lovely sight?
ALICE. Yes. But I'm afraid he'll catch cold lying on the damp
grass.
TWEEDLEDEE. He's dreaming now, and what do you think he's
dreaming about?
ALICE. Nobody can guess that.
TWEEDLEDEE. He's dreaming about you. And if he left off
dreaming about you, where do you suppose you'd be?
ALICE. Where I am now, of course.
TWEEDLEDEE. You'd be nowhere. Why you're only a sort of
thing in his dream. If he were to wake, you'd go out — Whhh! —
like a candle.
ALICE. I shouldn't! Besides, if *I'm* only a sort of thing in his
dream, what are you then?
TWEEDLEDEE. Ditto!

(*TWEEDLEDUM awakens.*)

TWEEDLEDEE & TWEEDLEDUM. (*giggle, then sing*) Hee hee hee
hee hee!
I KNOW WHAT YOU'RE THINKING ABOUT
BUT IT ISN'T SO, NO HOW.
TWEEDLEDEE.
CONTRARIWISE, IF IT WAS SO IT MIGHT BE
TWEEDLEDUM.
AND IF IT WERE SO, IT WOULD BE;
TWEEDLEDEE & TWEEDLEDUM.
BUT AS IT ISN'T IT AIN'T.
THAT'S LOGIC.
ALICE. (*plaintively*)
I WAS THINKING

WHICH IS THE BEST WAY OUT OF THIS WOOD.
IT'S GETTING SO DARK.
WOULD YOU TELL ME PLEASE. (*Music out.*)

TWEEDLEDEE & TWEEDLEDUM. (*giggle*) Hee hee hee hee!
TWEEDLEDEE. Do you like poetry?
ALICE. (*hesitantly*) Yes, some poetry.
TWEEDLEDUM. What shall I recite for her?
TWEEDLEDEE. "The Walrus and the Carpenter" is the longest.
ALICE. Oh no!

[MUSIC NO. 31: THE WALRUS AND THE CARPENTER]

TWEEDLEDEE.
THE SUN WAS SHINING ON THE SEA.
SHINING WITH ALL ITS MIGHT.
IT DID ITS VERY BEST TO MAKE
THE BILLOWS SMOOTH AND BRIGHT.
AND THIS WAS ODD BECAUSE IT WAS
     TWEEDLEDEE & TWEEDLEDUM.
THE MIDDLE OF THE NIGHT.

(*During the song the COMPANY can pantomime the story.*)

MEN.
THE WALRUS AND THE CARPENTER
WERE WALKING CLOSE AT HAND
THEY WEPT LIKE ANYTHING TO SEE
SUCH QUANTITIES OF SAND.
"IF THIS WERE ONLY CLEARED AWAY,"
THEY SAID, "IT WOULD BE . . .
     COMPANY.
GRAND!"

MEN.
"O OYSTERS, COME AND WALK WITH US,"
THE WALRUS DID BESEECH.
"A PLEASANT WALK, A PLEASANT TALK
ALONG THE BRINY BEACH.
WE CANNOT DO WITH MORE THAN FOUR
TO GIVE A HAND TO . . .
     COMPANY.
EACH!"

COMPANY.
"THE TIME HAS COME," THE WALRUS SAID,
"TO TALK OF MANY THINGS:
OF SHOES AND SHIPS AND SEALING WAX.
OF CABBAGES AND KINGS,
AND WHY THE SEA IS BOILING HOT,
AND WHETHER PIGS HAVE WINGS."
Oink! Oink!
MEN.
"BUT WAIT A BIT"
WOMEN.
"WAIT A BIT, WAIT A BIT!"
MEN.
THE OYSTERS CRIED.
WOMEN.
THE OYSTERS CRIED.
MEN.
"BEFORE WE HAVE OUR CHAT
FOR SOME OF US ARE OUT OF BREATH
AND ALL OF US ARE FAT!"
"NO HURRY" SAID THE CARPENTER,
THEY THANKED HIM MUCH FOR THAT.

"I WEEP FOR YOU"
COMPANY.
THE WALRUS SAID.
MEN.
"I DEEPLY SYMPATHIZE."
WITH SOBS AND TEARS HE SORTED OUT
THOSE OF THE LARGEST SIZE.
HOLDING HIS POCKET-HANDKERCHIEF
BEFORE HIS STREAMING EYE, EYE, EYE, EYE, EYES.

"O OYSTERS" SAID THE CARPENTER,
"WE'VE HAD A PLEASANT RUN.
SHALL WE BE TROTTING HOME AGAIN?"
BUT ANSWER CAME THERE NONE.
COMPANY.
AND THIS WAS SCARCELY ODD
BECAUSE THEY'D EATEN EVERY ONE.

(*EVERYONE CHORALE*)

COMPANY.
EATEN EVERY ONE
EVERY ONE,
EVERY ONE
EVERY ONE
EVERY ONE
THEY HAVE EATEN EATEN
EVERY ONE.

BASSES.	TENORS.	ALTOS.	SOPRANOS.
THEY'VE			
EATEN			
EVERY	THEY'VE		
ONE	EATEN		
EVERY	EVERY	THEY'VE	
ONE	ONE	EATEN	
EVERY	EVERY	EVERY	THEY'VE
ONE	ONE	ONE	EATEN
			EVERY
EVERY	EVERY	EVERY	ONE BE-
ONE	ONE	ONE	CAUSE
EVERY	EVERY	EVERY	THEY'VE
			EATEN
ONE	ONE	ONE	EVERY
EVERY	EVERY	EVERY	ONE
ONE	ONE	ONE	

MEN.
EVERY ONE, EVERY ONE
WOMEN.
EVERY ONE, EVERY ONE.
MEN.
EVERY ONE, EVERY ONE.
WOMAN.
EVERY ONE, EVERY ONE.
MEN & WOMEN.
EVERY ONE, EVERY ONE.
EVERY ONE, EVERY ONE.
EVERY ONE IS EATEN
EATEN EVERY ONE
THEY'VE EATEN
EATEN

EATEN
EATEN EVERY ONE BECAUSE THEY'VE
EATEN EVERY
ONE, EVERY ONE, EVERY ONE,
EVERY ONE, EVERY ONE.
ONE, ONE, ONE.
ONE, ONE, ONE.
ONE, ONE, EVERY ONE.

(*The COMPANY exits and leaves ALICE alone center stage. ALICE does the following dialogue by herself, changing her voice for the WHITE QUEEN's speeches.*)

ALICE. Am I addressing the White Queen?

[MUSIC NO. 32: THE WHITE QUEEN — UNDERSCORE]

QUEEN. Well, yes, if you call that a dressing. It isn't my notion of the thing at all.

ALICE. If your majesty would only tell me the right way to begin, I'll do it as well as I can.

QUEEN. But I don't want it done at all. I've been addressing myself for the last two hours.

ALICE. She's a terrible mess, and she's all over pins. May I put your shawl straight for you?

QUEEN. I don't know what's the matter with it. It's out of temper, I think. I've pinned it here, and I've pinned it there, but there's no pleasing it.

ALICE. Come. You look rather better now. But really, Your Majesty, you should have a lady's maid.

QUEEN. Oh really? Do you think so? Well, I would take you, then. I would take you with pleasure. O-o-oh! My finger is bleeding!

ALICE. What is the matter? Have you pricked your finger?

QUEEN. I haven't pricked it *yet*. But I soon shall.

ALICE. When do you expect to prick it?

QUEEN. When I fasten my shawl again. The brooch will come undone directly.

ALICE. Take care! You're holding it all crooked.

QUEEN. (*pricking her finger*) There, you see. That accounts for the bleeding. Now you understand the way things happen here.

ALICE. Why don't you scream now?

QUEEN. Why I've done all the screaming already. What would be the good of having it all over again?

ALICE. I don't understand you. It's dreadfully confusing.

QUEEN. That's the effect of living backwards. It always makes one a little giddy at first.

ALICE. Living backwards! I've never heard of such a thing!

QUEEN. But there's one great advantage in it, that one's memory works both ways.

ALICE. I'm sure mine only works one way. I can't remember things before they happen.

QUEEN. It's a poor sort of memory that only works one way. Why, I remember best, I remember best the things that happened the week after next. Only I wish I could manage to be glad. I never can remember the rule. You must be very happy, living in this wood, and being glad whenever you like.

ALICE. Only it is so very lonely here. (*She cries.*)

QUEEN. Shhhh. Shhhh. Oh, don't go on like that! Consider what a great girl you are. Consider what a long way you've come today. Consider what o'clock it is. Consider anything, only don't cry.

(*Music out. There is a pause. All the voices in the following dialogue come from offstage, except ALICE who remains center stage.*)

WOMAN 5. Can you keep from crying by considering things?

ALICE. Yes, that's the way it's done. Nobody can consider two things at once.

MAN 4. Let's consider your age to begin with. How old are you?

ALICE. Seven-and-a-half, exactly.

MAN 3. You needn't say "exactually." I can believe you without that.

WOMAN 5. Now I'll give you something to believe. I'm one hundred and one, five months and a day.

ALICE. I can't believe that.

WOMAN 2. Try again. Draw a long breath and shut your eyes.

ALICE. It's no use trying. I can't believe impossible things.

(*The WHITE KNIGHT appears stage left, pulling an imaginary horse after him.*)

KNIGHT. I daresay you haven't had much practice. When I was your age, I always did it for half-an-hour a day. Why, sometimes I've believed as many as six impossible things before breakfast. (*He mimes pulling the "horse" onstage.*) Come on, boy.

(*The "horse" refuses to budge. The KNIGHT keeps pulling and suddenly the "horse" moves, throwing the KNIGHT off balance. The KNIGHT brings the "horse" to center stage. Then he pets him, running his hand along the "horse's" back. The "horse" is abnormally tall and very long. The KNIGHT then attempts to mount the "horse" which keeps moving away from him and throwing him off balance. Finally, he watches the "horse" leave the playing area.*)

KNIGHT. He'll be back.

[MUSIC NO. 33: THE WHITE KNIGHT]

KNIGHT.
I SEE YOU'RE ADMIRING MY LITTLE BOX.
IT'S MY OWN INVENTION
TO KEEP CLOTHES AND SANDWICHES IN.

(*Throughout the song, ALICE and the KNIGHT mime the items mentioned.*)

ALICE.
WHAT KIND OF SANDWICHES?
KNIGHT.
YOU SEE I CARRY IT UPSIDE-DOWN,
SO THAT THE RAIN CAN'T GET IN.
ALICE.
BUT THE THINGS CAN GET OUT.
DON'T YOU KNOW THE LID'S OPEN?
KNIGHT.
I DIDN'T KNOW IT.
THEN ALL THE THINGS MUST HAVE FALLEN OUT.
AND THE BOX IS NO USE WITHOUT THEM.
ALICE.
NO, THE BOX IS NO USE WITHOUT THEM.

KNIGHT.
I'M GOING TO HANG MY BOX FROM A TREE,
CAN YOU GUESS WHY I DID THAT?

ALICE.
NO.

KNIGHT.
IN HOPES SOME BEES MAY MAKE A NEST IN IT,
THEN I SHOULD GET THE HONEY.

ALICE. (*She is humoring him now.*)
BUT YOU'VE GOT A BEEHIVE
OR SOMETHING LIKE ONE,
FASTENED TO THE SADDLE.

KNIGHT.
YES, IT'S A VERY GOOD BEEHIVE.
ONE OF THE BEST KIND.
BUT NOT A SINGLE BEE HAS COME NEAR IT YET.
AND THE OTHER THING IS A MOUSE-TRAP.

ALICE.
I WAS WONDERING WHAT THE MOUSE-TRAP WAS
    FOR.
IT ISN'T VERY LIKELY THERE WOULD BE MANY MICE
ON YOUR HORSE'S BACK.

KNIGHT.
YOU SEE, IT'S AS WELL TO BE PROVIDED
FOR EVERYTHING.
THAT'S THE REASON MY HORSE HAS ALL THOSE
ANKLETS 'ROUND HIS FEET.

ALICE.
BUT WHAT ARE THEY FOR?

KNIGHT.
TO GUARD AGAINST THE BITES OF SHARKS.

ALICE.
AH HA!

KNIGHT.
IT'S AN INVENTION OF MY OWN.
AND NOW HELP ME ON.
I'LL GO WITH YOU TO THE END
OF THE WOOD.
WHAT'S THAT DISH FOR?

ALICE.
IT'S MEANT FOR PLUMCAKE.

KNIGHT.
WE'D BETTER TAKE IT WITH US.

ALICE.
YES.
KNIGHT.
IT'LL COME IN HANDY
KNIGHT & ALICE.
IF WE FIND ANY PLUMCAKE.
KNIGHT.
I HOPE YOU'VE GOT YOUR HAIR WELL FASTENED ON.
ALICE.
ONLY IN THE USUAL WAY.
KNIGHT.
THAT'S HARDLY ENOUGH.
YOU SEE THE WIND IS SO
VERY STRONG HERE.
IT'S AS STRONG AS SOUP.
ALICE. Soup!
HAVE YOU MANAGED
A PLAN FOR KEEPING
THE HAIR FROM BEING
BLOWN OFF?
KNIGHT.
NOT YET.
BUT I'VE GOT A PLAN
FOR KEEPING IT FROM FALLING OFF.
ALICE.
I SHOULD LIKE TO HEAR IT.
KNIGHT.

FIRST YOU TAKE AN	ALICE.
UPRIGHT STICK	FIRST YOU TAKE AN
THEN YOU MAKE YOUR	UPRIGHT STICK
HAIR CREEP UP IT	CREEP UP IT
LIKE A FRUIT TREE.	LIKE A FRUIT TREE?

KNIGHT.
NOW THE REASON HAIR FALLS OFF
IS BECAUSE IT HANGS DOWN.
THINGS NEVER FALL UPWARDS
YOU KNOW.
ALICE.
I KNOW.
KNIGHT.
IT'S A PLAN OF MY OWN
INVENTION

YOU MAY TRY IT IF YOU
  LIKE.
IT'S A PLAN OF MY OWN
  INVENTION . . .

ALICE.
IT'S A PLAN OF MY OWN
  INVENTION
I MAY TRY IT IF I LIKE.
IT'S A PLAN OF MY OWN
  INVENTION

(*KNIGHT loses his concentration and pauses.*)

KNIGHT. I'm going to sing you a song to comfort you.

ALICE. Oh no. It is very long?

KNIGHT. Yes, but it's very, very beautiful. Everyone that hears me sing it, either it brings tears into their eyes or else . . .

ALICE. Or else what?

KNIGHT. Or else it doesn't. The name of the song is called "Haddock's Eyes."

ALICE. Oh, that's the name of the song, is it?

KNIGHT. No, you don't understand. That's what the name of the song is *called.* The name really is "The Aged Man."

ALICE. Then I ought to have said, "That's what the song is called?"

KNIGHT. No, that's quite another thing. The song is called "Ways and Means" but that's not what the song *is.*

ALICE. What *is* the song then?

KNIGHT. It was getting to that. The song really is "A-Sitting On A Gate." And the tune is my own invention.

[MUSIC NO. 34: AN AGED, AGED MAN]

KNIGHT.
I'LL TELL THEE EVERYTHING I CAN
THERE'S LITTLE TO RELATE . . .
(*He suddenly can't remember words and pauses.*)

ALICE.
. . . I SAW AN AGED, AGED MAN
A-SITTING ON A GATE.
"WHO ARE YOU, AGED MAN?" I SAID,
"AND HOW IS IT YOU LIVE?"
HIS ANSWERS TRICKLED THROUGH MY HEAD,
LIKE WATER THROUGH A SIEVE.

HE SAID "I LOOK FOR BUTTERFLIES
THAT SLEEP AMONG THE WHEAT;

I MAKE THEM INTO MUTTON-PIES
AND SELL THEM IN THE STREET.
I SELL THEM UNTO MEN," HE SAID,
"WHO SAIL ON STORMY SEAS;
AND THAT'S THE WAY I GET MY BREAD,
A TRIFLE, IF YOU PLEASE."

(*Throughout song, KNIGHT does simple mime actions to imitate the story of the song.*)

HE SAID "I HUNT FOR HADDOCK'S EYES
AMONG THE HEATHER BRIGHT,
AND WORK THEM INTO WAISTCOAT-BUTTONS
IN THE SILENT NIGHT.
I THANKED HIM MUCH FOR TELLING ME
THE WAY HE GOT HIS WEALTH,
BUT CHIEFLY FOR HIS WISH THAT HE
MIGHT DRINK MY NOBLE HEALTH.

AND NOW, IF E'ER BY CHANCE I PUT
MY FINGERS INTO GLUE,
OR MADLY SQUEEZE A RIGHT-HAND FOOT
INTO A LEFT-HAND SHOE,
OR IF I DROP UPON MY TOE
A VERY HEAVY WEIGHT,
I WEEP, FOR IT REMINDS ME SO
OF THAT OLD MAN I USED TO KNOW,
WHOSE LOOK WAS MILD, WHOSE SPEECH WAS SLOW,
WHOSE HAIR WAS WHITER THAN THE SNOW,
WHOSE FACE WAS VERY LIKE A CROW,
WITH EYES, LIKE CINDERS, ALL AGLOW,
WHO SEEMED DISTRACTED WITH HIS WOE,
WHO ROCKED HIS BODY TO AND FRO,
AND MUTTERED MUMBLINGLY AND LOW,
AS IF HIS MOUTH WERE FULL OF DOUGH,
THAT SUMMER EVENING LONG AGO.
A-SITTING ON A GATE.

(*KNIGHT's "horse" is again suddenly present, he goes to it, grabs its reins and starts to pull it offstage, but stops.*)

KNIGHT. (*to ALICE*) By the by. It's only a few more yards,

across the creek and over the hill, and you'll be a Queen.
ALICE. A Queen?
KNIGHT. Yes, but. (*"Horse" starts to pull him offstage.*) Whoa! Be very . . . Whoa boy! (*He exits.*)

ALICE. A Queen! How grand it sounds! I never expected to be a Queen . . . so soon!

(*A roar of a lion is heard. UNICORN [MAN 1] and LION [MAN 4] enter. MAN 3 carries UNICORN's horn over UNICORN's head. MAN 5 carries crown over LION's head. They circle each other warily. A QUEEN [WOMAN 2] appears next to ALICE.*)

QUEEN. They're at it again.
ALICE. Who's at it again?
QUEEN. The Lion and the Unicorn, of course.
ALICE. Fighting for the crown?
QUEEN. To be sure. And the best of the joke is, that it's *your* crown all the while!

[MUSIC NO. 35: THE LION AND THE UNICORN.]

(*During the song, LION and UNICORN fight in slow motion.*)

QUEEN.
THE LION AND THE UNICORN
WERE FIGHTING FOR THE CROWN.
THE LION BEAT THE UNICORN
ALL AROUND THE TOWN.
SOME GAVE THEM WHITE BREAD,
SOME GAVE THEM BROWN.
SOME GAVE THEM PLUM-CAKE
AND DRUMMED THEM OUT OF TOWN.

(*LION and UNICORN stop fighting and stare at ALICE.*)

UNICORN. What is this?
LION. It is a child. We only found it today. It's as large as life, and twice as natural.
UNICORN. I always thought they were fabulous monsters. Is it alive?

ALICE. Yes.

LION. It can talk.

UNICORN. Talk, child.

ALICE. I always thought Unicorns were fabulous monsters. I never saw one until today.

UNICORN. Well, now that we have seen each other, if you'll believe in me, I'll believe in you. Is that a bargain?

ALICE. (*nods "yes"*)

[MUSIC NO. 36: WHAT THERE IS (REPRISE)]

(*ALICE and UNICORN kneel facing each other. MAN 5 sits crosslegged in the background holding crown, humming and improvising a raga in rough counterpoint to the following:*)

UNICORN.
IN THIS MY GREEN WORLD
FLOWERS, BIRDS ARE HANDS
THEY HOLD ME
I AM LOVED ALL DAY . . .

UNICORN & ALICE.
ALL THIS PLEASES ME
I AM AMUSED
I HAVE TO LAUGH FROM CRYING
TREES MOUNTAINS ARE ARMS
I AM LOVED ALL DAY . . .

CHILDREN GRASS ARE TEARS
I CRY
I AM LOVED ALL DAY . . .
EVERYTHING POMPOUS MAKES ME LAUGH
I AM AMUSED OFTEN ENOUGH
IN THIS MY BEAUTIFUL GREEN WORLD
OH THERE IS LOVE ALL DAY.

(*MAN 5 places crown on ALICE's head.*)

ALICE. Queen Alice Pleasance Liddell!

[MUSIC NO. 37: QUEEN ALICE]

(*COMPANY performs a regal procession with brightly colored banners. By the song's end ALICE is seated upstage center on a throne.*)

ALICE. (*shouts letters*)

A!

COMPANY.

A — A BOAT, BENEATH A SUNNY SKY.

ALICE.

L!

COMPANY.

L — LINGERING ONWARD DREAMILY.

ALICE.

I!

COMPANY.

I — IN AN EVENNG OF JULY.

ALICE.

C!

COMPANY.

C — CHILDREN THREE THAT NESTLE NEAR.

ALICE.

E!

COMPANY.

E — EAGER EYE AND WILLING EAR.

ALICE.

P!

COMPANY.

PLEASED A SIMPLE TALE TO HEAR.

L — LONG HAS PALED THAT SUNNY SKY

E — ECHOES FADE AND MEMORIES DIE.

A — AUTUMN FROSTS HAVE SLAIN JULY.

S — STILL SHE HAUNTS ME PHANTOM-WISE

A — ALICE MOVING UNDER SKIES,

N — NEVER SEEN BY WAKING EYES.

C — CHILDREN YET, THE TALE TO HEAR.

E — EAGER EYE AND WILLING EAR.

L — LOVINGLY SHALL NESTLE NEAR.

I — IN A WONDERLAND THEY LIE.

D — DREAMING AS THE DAYS GO BY,

D — DREAMING AS THE SUMMERS DIE:

E — EVERY DRIFTING DOWN THE STREAM

L — LINGERING IN THE GOLDEN GEALM —

L—LIFE WHAT IS IT BUT A
L—LIFE WHAT IS IT BUT A
L—LIFE WHAT IS IT BUT A DREAM?

(*The COMPANY moves slowly to their original seated positions on the platform. ALICE removes crown and sits at platform center, asleep, leaning on EDITH to her right as at the beginning of the show.*)

[MUSIC NO. 38: WHAT IS A LETTER?]

(*Guitar vamps under the following dialogue.*)

EDITH. Alice! Alice, wake up, it's time for your lesson.

ALICE. You've woken me from a very pleasant dream.

EDITH. I'm sure it was a lovely dream, dear. But it's time for your lesson now. (*She sings.*)
WHAT IS A LETTER?

ALICE.
THE GUARDIAN OF HISTORY.

EDITH.
WHAT IS A WORD?

ALICE.
THE SPOKESMAN FOR THE MIND.

EDITH.
WHAT MAKES A WORD?

ALICE.
THE TONGUE.

EDITH.
WHAT IS THE TONGUE?

ALICE.
THE WHIP OF THE AIR.

EDITH.
WHAT IS THE AIR?

ALICE.
THE GUARDIAN OF LIFE.

EDITH.
WHAT IS LIFE?

ALICE.
THE JOY OF THE BLESSED.
THE SORROW OF THE MISERABLE.
THE EXPECTATION OF DEATH.

EDITH.
WHAT IS DEATH?
ALICE.
THE TEARS OF THE LIVING.
THE THIEF OF A MAN.
EDITH.
WHAT IS MAN?
ALICE.
A GUEST OF THIS EARTH.
I SAW A WOMAN FLYING
WEARING A BEAK OF IRON.
AND A WOODEN BODY
AND A FEATHERED TAIL.
EDITH.
THAT IS THE ARROW
THE COMPANION OF SOLDIERS.
ALICE.
NOT A BIRD?
EDITH.
NOT A BIRD.
COMPANY.
NOT A BIRD.
EDITH.
WHAT IS A BIRD?
ALICE.
THE GIVER OF SONG.
EDITH.
WHAT IS THE SONG?
ALICE.
THE SPOKESMAN OF THE SOUL.
EDITH.
WHAT IS THE SOUL?
ALICE.
THE SPIRIT OF LIFE.
COMPANY.
WHAT IS LIFE?
THE JOY OF THE BLESSED.
THE SORROW OF THE MISERABLE.
THE EXPECTATION OF DEATH.
WHAT IS DEATH?
THE TEARS OF THE LIVING.

THE THIEF OF A MAN.
WHAT IS MAN?
  ALICE.
A GUEST ON THIS EARTH.

(*COMPANY pick up their bells, which have been positioned
  behind them on the platform, and ring them in unison:*)

[MUSIC NO. 39: BOWS]

QUESTIONS & EXERCISES

1. In a few words, describe your favorite character in "Alice At the Palace." Then relate an incident in your life which is similar to one experienced by the character.

2. What is your favorite song in the program? What is your favorite dance sequence?

3. How would you answer the Caterpillar's question, "Who are you?"

4. Alice grows smaller, and then wonders if this change means she will not get any older. Would you like to stay the same size and age you are now? Why or why not?

5. What is your opinion of the Queen who claims "I am absolutely perfect"? Do you know anyone who believes he or she is perfect?

6. Alice is invited to a croquet game which is played with hedgehogs and flamingos. What is the silliest game you have ever played?

7. What does the Mock Turtle mean when he says, "A wise fish never goes anywhere without a porpoise"?

8. Why do Alice and the Jabberwock fight? How does Alice react after the battle?

9. Is there any day recently when you have felt that your surroundings were becoming, in Alice's words, "curioser and curioser"? Share your story with the group.

10. Alice tells the White Knight: "I can't believe impossible things." Have you ever believed in an impossible thing and discovered that it was true?

11. After talking with Alice, the Unicorn concludes that children are "fabulous monsters." What does he mean?

12. Alice is very happy when she learns that she can be a queen. Make a list of three things you would do if you were a King or Queen. Compare you list to those of other members of your group. Do you have similar goals?

13. What do you think Alice learns from her experiences?